Passage to America
Adjustment of Status

by M.C. Deman and C.R. Joyce

DORRANCE PUBLISHING CO
EST. 1920
PITTSBURGH, PENNSYLVANIA 15238

Dorrance Publishing Co
585 Alpha Drive
Pittsburgh, PA 15238
Visit our website at *www.dorrancebookstore.com*

ISBN: 978-1-4809-9419-5
eISBN: 978-1-4809-8571-1

Table of Contents

Chapter 1: The Immigrants

A herd of wildebeests meander through the great expanse like a winding river, flowing as one, not a single creature distinguishable from the next. As individuals, they are inherently chaotic and wild, trampling each other and fighting along the way. As a herd, from a distance, their migration appears calculated, organized and unstoppable. Staying close to the herd protects each creature from hungry predators. Together, they push toward better lands to feed and flourish as a species. Horns blaring, black carbon emissions rising, patience tested, Kathrina and her family sit in a cab in traffic on their way to the airport. The herd is analogous to the seemingly never-ending traffic in the streets of Manila. Smog replaces dust; aggressive drivers of cars, trucks, bikes, jeepneys, tricycles, busses and pedicabs replace wildebeest; and corrupt Manila Pulis replace hungry predators. The contrasts don't stop there; Kathrina and her family are on their way to the airport to travel to the "Land of the Free and the Home of the Brave," the United States of America, a nation under God, blessed and akin to the land of the Canaanites in the Bible, flowing with milk and honey. Kathrina's father planned this trip, having applied for visitors' visas months ago. The family will travel to the States and stay with his sister during the visit. Everyone in the family believes this trip to be a vacation; secretly however, Kathrina's father has intentions to do more than simply visit. He has witnessed his sister, having lived in the States for over a decade, experience a drastic change in quality of life. Growing older, with limited options for advancing his family financially, he has made a unilateral executive action to uproot his family from Manila and take his chance at getting a share of the "milk and honey."

Kathrina, a month from her 18th birthday, is fortunate to have the opportunity to go on this trip. Despite the efforts of her father, her elder sister's visa was denied by the U.S. Embassy in Manila. As an adult and the single mother of a young child, she was lacking a source of verifiable income and significant property. She was deemed a risk for overstaying her visa and was left to be the caretaker of the family home.

Sitting in the back of the cab, Kathrina's mind is moving at warp speed as she imagines what to expect when she arrives in America. She fantasizes about visiting Disneyland, standing in the footsteps of celebrities at the Chinese Theater in Hollywood, trekking down the walk of fame, California sunsets, and visiting iconic places from America's greatest commercial for tourism: television and the movies. She is equally excited to connect with her cousins, who are like celebrities themselves when they come to visit the Philippines for holidays. She has remained in touch with them over the years via chat and social media. The picture they paint of life in America is as foreign to her as life on Mars. The thought of computers and wireless Internet in almost every home, online shopping, streaming music and movies, access to affordable health care and government welfare creates visions of some futuristic utopia.

Growing more and more anxious each moment in traffic, Kathrina inquires, "Papa, how much longer? When will we be in America?"

Her dad, equally anxious and annoyed by the cab driver's poor driving, grunts, "Kathrina, relax. Tuesday at eleven am."

Confused, Kathrina replies, "But Papa today is Tuesday! It's going to take a week?"

Her dad now laughing, "California is a day behind us, so we will be traveling back in time."

Walking through the airport, they reach the summit of excitement and anticipation as the reality has set in that they are on their way to America. Endless lines of travelers might discourage someone on their way to an undesirable destination, but for someone traveling to America, these lines add fuel to the excitement. Across from their departure gate there is a McDonald's; Kathrina wonders if McDonald's in America is different.

Kathrina's dad notices her staring in the direction of the golden arches and makes a proposal, "Let's have some McDonald's. We need to practice being American!" He takes the lead and orders Big Macs and cokes as a preface to their American journey, this meal essentially being an appetizer to the entrée they will consume in America. By the time they are done eating, it's time to board their plane.

Kathrina, sitting across the aisle from her parents, is a little worried. This being her first time flying, she is in amazed that something so large and heavy could actually fly. In an instance, every movie with a catastrophic plane crash cycles through her mind. The plane taxis while the flight crew demonstrates the safety equipment and gives instructions to follow in the event of an emergency. Their voices like white noise are unintelligible as she is in a fog trying to relax and calm her nerves. As the jet engines power up for takeoff, Kathrina's death grip on the arm rests gets tighter and tighter. Her eyes are closed as the plane shoots down the runway, the gentleman sitting next to her notices her distress.

He speaks to her with a foreign accent, "Ma'am are you ok?" Hearing his voice brings her out of the fog. She looks to him and the fear is evident in her eyes. He continues, "I fly between LAX and Manila every week. Don't be afraid. The rumbling, the vibrations, it's all normal." She listens but what he has said hasn't really sunk in because she is distracted by his American English accent. It takes her full concentration to follow his conversation as she translates each word in her mind. The gentleman explains he is a Christian missionary and offers to say a prayer of comfort with her. She closes her eyes and focuses on the voice of the missionary as he prays, asking God to comfort her and to keep her safe during her travels. As the missionary says amen, the plane has taken off and is climbing to cruising altitude. Kathrina smiles and thanks the gentleman. Having spent the entire night before the trip tossing and turning, Kathrina is exhausted. The vibrations and low rumble of the jet engine are a natural sleep aid. Within minutes, Kathrina is in a deep dreamless sleep only to awaken upon touchdown at LAX.

At baggage claim, Kathrina and her family are reunited with her aunt and cousins. There is no short supply of hugs and tears of happiness as they have completed the migration. Like wildebeest quenching their thirst at the first watering hole in a new land, they stand waiting for their bags around the luggage carousel. Once their bags are collected and the family is regrouped, they pile into Tita Eileen's minivan and begin their ride home. Her van instantly transforms into a chartered tour bus; Kathrina's eyes are immediately transfixed on the sites of Los Angeles. Leaving the airport, she's impressed that every car looks new. The public landscaping is neatly manicured and the roads maintained. Traffic is organized and drivers follow the directions of streetlights. People communicate with signal indicators, rather than blaring horns and aggressive driving movements. There are people of all sizes, shapes and colors: people who look like the athletes on her favorite basketball teams; people who look like the folks in *Friends* on her favorite TV show; people who look like the dancers and singers in her favorite pop music videos; people who look like they come from exotic lands dressed in their traditional garb; and people who look like her. Before merging onto the highway to head to the valley, Tita Eileen promises a special treat. Off in the distance, a large brown disk is barely noticeable to Kathrina. As they close the distance, it gets larger and larger; the shape begins to take form. Kathrina exclaims, "Papa, it's a donut?" Tita Eileen and her cousins are laughing to the point of tears and Eileen says, "Yes Kathy, that's my 'welcome to USA' treat. We will stop for coffee and donuts at Randy's. You will love it!"

Making their way home through the city, Tita Eileen's van is full of excitement and wonder. Like the tram tour on the backlot at Universal Studios, they make brief stops at every possible attraction and Tita serves as the curator of each exhibition: Hollywood, Santa Monica Pier, Venice Beach, and Rodeo Drive in Beverly Hills. The experience is surreal and more vivid than Kathrina's greatest dreams and fantasies of America. Her appetite is barely whet by these appetizers; her excitement and hunger for more is difficult to contain.

Almost a month into the vacation and everyone is having so much fun. There have been multiple family get-togethers and barbeques, trips to Disneyland and Universal City Walk, picnics at the beach and in the mountains.

However, two weeks into the vacation, Kathrina notices that her dad has become an absentee vacationer. He's gone early in the mornings before they wake up and he often returns late at night after they have returned from their tourist activities. He's somewhat distant, but always in a very optimistic mood. Kathrina wonders what he could be doing all day, but she assumes that he is hanging out with old friends from his childhood. One evening he returns just in time for the family dinner. At the table, Kathrina and her cousins are a little down. The vibe is drab and there is a drought of smiles and laughter because everyone is conscious of the "elephant in the room:" visa expiration date is a week away. It is almost time to return to the Philippines. Kathrina's dad decides to lighten the mood; he inquires, "Kathrina, having you had enough of this place? Ready to return to our little island?"

Kathrina, feeling her dad is teasing, rolls her eyes and says, "Papa! It's so wonderful here." Her dad responds with a grin that would put the Cheshire cat to shame and states, "Ok, we will stay." Tita Eileen and her mom begin laughing hysterically because of the look on Kathrina's face. Her face is confused, her facial muscles trying to form a smile, but reason tells her it cannot be true. She is stuck, hanging on to his last word: stay. She tunes out the laughter from everyone around her and now with a serious disposition, inquires, "Stay? What do you mean Papa?" At this point her dad stands and walks over to her. He grabs her hand and proceeds to explain that he and Tita Eileen had been planning this trip for a long time. With sincerity and humility in his voice, he explains that he couldn't offer her much of a future in Manila and that he wants the best for his family. Like any father, he wants her to have the best education and the opportunity to fulfill her greatest dreams. He kisses her on the forehead and continues, "This is our home now. I already have a job. I've been working to secure this for you, for our family." Suddenly, the sound of laughs from peanut gallery has morphed into the sound of sniffing noses like those a proud mom might make at a wedding.

Eager to acclimate herself to the American way of life, Kathrina makes efforts to connect to fellow friends who have completed the migrant journey. She reconnects with a childhood friend who has started her first year in a nursing program at UCLA. Her friend Arlene works as hard as she plays. Kathrina, curious to experience college life in America, begins spending weekend after weekend at the UCLA campus. She dreams of attending University herself but knows that her father struggles to put food on the table. At a UCLA basketball game, Arlene's boyfriend Julius introduces Kathrina to his best friend David. David comes from a very affluent family back in the Philippines. He travels to America like a migratory flock of birds, returning to the Philippines at the end of the grueling Filipino summers. Kathrina and David instantly connect, both having grown up in the same district in Manila they have a lot in common and the four-some of friends grow very close. Kathrina and David are inseparable like lovebirds and soon David too is an undocumented immigrant. He has overstayed his visa and is depending on the financial support of his father back in the Philippines. The couple aspires to gain independence so that they can seriously consider starting a life together.

Kathrina, wanting to help her Papa with the bills and to establish her independence, asks her Tita Eileen to help her find a job. Eileen introduces Kathrina to her friend Caroline who works as a RN. Caroline has a reputation for helping connect Filipino domestic caregivers with patients she has treated at the hospital. One of Caroline's current patients is the sickly wife of an elderly, semi-retired writer. With her declining health and his age, she is certain that Kathrina can help them. Caroline makes the introduction and Kathrina starts her career as a live-in domestic caregiver the following week with the hopes there will be a place for David.

Soon her life becomes a repeating cycle, a routine, and after 10 years she is no closer to attaining the American dream…

Chapter 2: An Awakening

It's early on a cold Sunday morning and sunrays are beaming through the blinds. Her face awash in the warm radiance of the sun, Kathrina rises from her slumber anxious to spend the day realizing dreams of happiness with her love, David. She rolls over to wake David with a soft gentle kiss but finds nothing but a cold pillow by her side. She slides out of the bed, rubbing her eyes and curious to find out what could have summoned David away from her side prior to the sun's rise. As she walks down the hall toward the living room, she can hear David speaking over the sound of gunshots, explosions, and screaming voices. As she enters the family room, she discovers David fully engaged in an online video game battle. He is playing a game he purchased the day before entitled "Call of Duty." She calls out to him, "Good morning babe." He doesn't respond. She speaks louder, "Good morning babe!" Again, no response. She approaches and stands in front of the TV to get David's attention. Now he exclaims with a piercing tone, "Oh no, you'll get me killed! Move Please!"

Kathrina, now hurt and feeling marginalized by the attention David is giving a video game, walks away with her shoulders slumped. She stops at the bar in the kitchen to grab her freshly-charged mobile phone and retreats to the kitchen to warm some fresh pan de sal and to make coffee. While her bread is warming, she notices that she has several notifications from her Facebook and Viber chat applications, so she begins to scroll through and read while placing a K-Cup in the Keurig. She discovers her close friend Arlene has sent her a number of messages on Viber asking her why she hasn't commented on or liked the photos that she has recently posted on Facebook of her on a date the night before with Ranjith, her new crush. The toaster bell dings and the aroma of fresh pan de sal fills the room as she opens the toaster door. She butters the bread, grabs her coffee and sits comfortably on a stool at the kitchen bar. She lifts her coffee to take a sip and her face is teased by the fragrant steam. Her eyes widen and she begins to browse through the photos that Arlene has posted. She can't help but to think how Arlene has connected with an Indian guy almost 10 years her junior. She never would have thought that Arlene, coming from such a traditional and old-fashioned Pinoy family, would consider dating out of her culture. However, as she glances over the pictures and reads the captions the words though, *eloquent* and *sweet* do no justice in expressing the sheer joy and happiness evident in both of their faces. The kisses, the hugs, the smiles could sell even the lamest Hallmark Valentines greeting cards. Kathrina, though happy for her friend, has a sudden mix of emotions with envy rising to the top. She begins to think of a sweet and thoughtful response to write in the Facebook feed, when David sneaks up behind her and like a kid starts pressing buttons on her phone while asking what happened to his bread and coffee. Kathrina doesn't say a word, but the look in her eyes cuts deep so David just giggles and walks away to prepare his breakfast. Kathrina begins to like and craft responses to each of the photos in the feed: "You guys look happy;" "Aww too cute;" "Love is in the air;" and teasingly "Arlene and Ranjith sitting in a tree, K-I-S-S-I-N-G." She giggles, but simultaneously a tear drops from her eye.

Both having their fill of coffee and pan de sal, they move to the bathroom to get ready for the day. While David is in the shower, Kathrina begins to brush her teeth and then her hair. David in the shower is playing his favorite Red Hot Chili Peppers song. "Give it away now, give away now...." He's in total rock-out mode singing along to the lyrics of "Give it away" as if Anthony Kiedis wrote the song exclusively for him. Kathrina exclaims, "DAVID! I'm here too!" He replies, "Well then sing along." Patience fading, she screams, "Turn that shit off! I want to talk to you. What are we doing today? We should do something romantic and fun."

After a seemingly long moment of silence, David peaks out from behind the shower curtain and says, "I have a basketball game with the guys today at 1. I thought you would want to come cheer us on. Afterwards, we can go to the mall because I want to get the expansion pack for "Call of Duty" and then we can go to that shoe store you like and maybe eat in the food court too." Happy to just leave the house, Kathrina affirms his plans with a small smile and shrug of the shoulders.

At the basketball game Kathrina sits with all the other wives and girl-friends. They are all excited to cheer for their men who have made it to the league playoffs. There is an elevated tension and stress in the air because the ladies know that the outcome of this game could result in a rough evening as they struggle to comfort their "boys" after such a hard-fought season. Just before tip-off, David comes over to Kathrina to solicit a good luck kiss and she generously obliges. As the game gets underway, the ladies begin to discuss their week in review. With excitement, Stephanie announces that she is two months pregnant. After a round of congratulations and discussion about the sex of the baby and potential names, Ruby strategically picks her moment to announce that Ryan has proposed to her and that they are going to get married in June. Angelina chimes in that she and Rick have closed escrow on their dream home in Manhattan Beach, CA and invites everyone to their housewarming party. Kathrina, secretly growing envious and feeling left out, looks up and realizes its already nearly halftime. She checks the score, realizes their men are losing badly and are beginning to look defeated, so she interrupts all the boasting and rallies the ladies to begin cheering their men on, "Let's go team Ginebra! You can do it."

At halftime, Kathrina notices that most of the guys come over to the bleachers to receive comforting words of encouragement from their women, while David sits sulking in anger on the bench. She overhears Ryan telling Ruby that he is proud to have such a beautiful woman cheering for him. Angelina updates Rick that she has invited the ladies to their housewarming party. He enthusiastically, starts telling everyone about the home's features, the bonus appliances, the swimming pool and guesthouse, and most importantly, the close proximity to the beach so that he can surf in the mornings before work.

Suddenly, David yells out to the guys and calls for a team meeting. As the men begrudgingly retreat to the bench, they have to endure David barking orders about what needs to be done to win the game; Kathrina feels a little less significant and wonders what she has done wrong. What happened to her great American ambitions? As the game continues, she sits quietly and listens to the other ladies continue discussing all the happy announcements about their lives. She tries to distract herself by browsing through her social media feeds, but even there she is overwhelmed by the stories of success and happiness. Given her current status in America, she knows that she is limited to living vicariously. Looking through the feed she imagines it's her posing in front of her new luxury car; it's her snorkeling at the Great Barrier Reef in Australia; it's her posting an evite for a dinner party at her home in the Hollywood Hills. A battle between realism and optimism has commenced as she contemplates her relationship with David.

As Kathrina watches the clock tick down in the game, she is reminded how time is running out in her pursuit of happiness. Luckily though, team Ginebra has come back and notched a win worthy of celebration. All the guys are excited, and the wives rush over to congratulate their men. Kathrina gathers her things and walks over, unhurried, to join in the festive excitement of reaching the league finals. David is ecstatic and without thinking, reaches to caress Kathrina, but she pulls away disgusted by his sweat and gives him a cold high-five. She tells him good job and asks him to quickly get cleaned up and changed so that they can get over to the mall.

After several hours of debating which stores to visit first, David and Kathrina have worked up an appetite and head to the food court. Their mouths watering from the mix of appetizing aromas, David is the first to suggest what to eat. He exclaims, "Supersize me! Let's get Mc Do to go because 'Call of Duty' is waiting." Kathrina with disgust shrieks, "Putang ina mo!!! I wanted to sit and enjoy a date night with you at the Cheesecake Factory. I'm craving the salmon and asparagus. Come on, let's enjoy a real meal."

In the midst of their dispute, Kathrina sees a familiar face out of the corner of her eye. She nudges David aside and calls out, "Jennifer, oh my God what are you doing here?" Jennifer replies, "I brought the kids to get new school clothes. Carl and I just got back from his deployment to Germany and the kids are starting school on Monday. It feels so good to be home again and what a treat it is to run into you. We need to catch up. Let's exchange numbers and catch up soon." The two exchange numbers and Kathrina says, "I can't wait!" As Kathrina begins to turn to walk away, Jennifer says, "Wait, aren't you going to introduce me to your friend?" Kathrina apologizes and says, "This is my boyfriend, David. We've been dating for 11 years now. David, this is an old friend from high school; her name is Jennifer." David extends a hand and says, "It's a pleasure to meet you." Jennifer becomes distracted by the kids and responds with, "Goodbye I've got to run the kids have already begun to lose patience." Kathrina turns back to David and says, "There is no way I'm eating McDonalds for dinner; can we at least eat here at the Mongolian grill?"

As they are walking back to the mall parking lot, David begs Kathrina to drive home. Rubbing his tummy, he yawns huge and says, "I feel a food coma coming on." Kathrina rolls her eyes and takes the keys. As soon as she gets into the car and begins to adjust her seat, David's eyes are already closing. David is already snoring as she reaches the first stoplight. As David enters dreamland, Kathrina is on autopilot. Without thought, she plots a route home; there is music playing but she isn't listening. Her mind is moving at the speed of light as she begins to reminisce of her school days and her close friendship with Jennifer. Her mind plays back memories of their dreams of immigrating to the U.S. in pursuit of the great American Dream. During late-night study breaks they would watch TV shows like *Baywatch, Beverly Hills 902010* and classic *Beverly Hillbillies*. Watching these shows gave them glimpses of a quality of life unlike any they could ever imagine experiencing in the Philippines. They would joke each night about becoming mail-order brides in exchange for the opportunity to sunbathe on Los Angeles beaches and to rub elbows with the celebrities and socialites they saw on TV. Kathrina has been driving for nearly 40 minutes to get home and is so disconnected from reality that she misses her exit from the freeway. She shouts in disgust and David is abruptly awakened from his powernap, "What what, where are we?" Rubbing his eyes, he asks "Where are you going? You missed our exit?" Annoyed, she exits and makes her way home.

The moment the couple walks through their front door, David is already making a beeline for PS4 to get online and try out the expansion pack. Kathrina makes her way to shower and freshen up before heading to bed. Each day she grows a little wearier with the path she has chosen for her life. She is overwhelmed with depression and begins to feel anxious about how the future will unfold. As she steps into the shower, the warm steam enters her lungs. As she lathers, the fragrant lavender in her shower gel is intensified by the steam. The aroma soothes her troubled soul and the hot water relaxes the tension that has been building in her muscles throughout the day. As she turns away from the water to shampoo her hair, she closes her eyes, puts her head directly under the flowing water and forgets her worries. For a brief moment there isn't a worry in her mind and she is at peace. She begins to wonder and contemplate what her old friend Jennifer has been up to over the years. Who is this guy, Carl? Their lives diverged after boarding school, yet by chance they have crossed paths again. What must it be like for Jennifer to have two kids and travel the world with her military husband? Is there something that she can learn from Jennifer's experience? Is Jennifer happy? Mid-thought, she is shaken by banging on the door and she is rudely brought back to reality by David demanding, "Hey I need to take a shit!"

Chapter 3: The Conversation

Now in bed, Kathrina's curiosities about Jennifer have grown into a hunger that must be fed before she can even think about sleeping. She reaches for her phone and decides to give Jennifer a call. Jennifer answers on the first ring and says, "Perfect timing, the kids have just gone to sleep. Carl is working a night shift at the base, so we have all night to catch up!" Kathrina giggles and queries, "Like our late-night study sessions in school? Should I make some ramen and coffee?" The two old friends laugh out loud.

There is a brief moment of silence as both of them have so many questions and don't know where to start. At the same time, they ask how did you meet Carl/David? Kathrina, still angry with David interrupting her shower, she exclaims, "You go! Tell me how you and Carl met." Jennifer explains that Carl had just finished Airforce basic training and that he was assigned to a special unit tasked with training the Philippine Airforce at Clark Air Base. Given the close proximity to Manila, many of the airmen would spend their recreational time partying and shopping in Manila. During a weekend break, Carl planned a weekend getaway to the Manila Peninsula hotel.

She continues to explain that she had gone through one of the busiest and most draining weeks ever at work and she had decided to meet up with a girlfriend at the bar in the Peninsula. Jennifer tells Kathrina, "Just as I raise my cocktail to toast my friend Theresa, I see a tall dark figure walk into the dim lighted bar area. I froze, and Theresa started laughing at me."

Jennifer continues, "After having two more cocktails and gossiping about people at work, Theresa noticed that I was totally distracted by this guy sitting in the corner all by himself. Theresa dared me to go over and introduce myself. Having never spoken to a black guy before, I was hesitant. But, by this time I had plenty of liquid courage and he was really cute. He had already smiled at me several times between his glances at his mobile phone and drinking his beer. I walked over and simply said, 'Hi my name is Jennifer,' and from there we haven't looked back. In fact, Theresa got bored and left early because Carl and I were immediately enraptured with each other.

"Carl and I quickly became the closest of friends and soon after, lovers. We would stay up at night on the phone until we were both falling asleep. We would text throughout the day endlessly. Anything more than an hour gap in communication felt like days. How lucky and blessed I am to find a man who I could love, who loved me, and could possibly provide a path to my citizenship in the U.S. We dated regularly for the entire two years of his deployment to Clark Air base and at the end he proposed to me and we filed for a fiancé visa so that I could travel with him."

Kathrina interjectes: "You are so brave. Have you had any second thoughts or regrets?"

Jennifer responds in a strong affirmative, "Not one! I wish I'd met him earlier in my life. We got married on his first leave back to the States and I got to meet his family and tour all over California for almost a month before his next deployment, which was to France. It's such a romantic country. I blame France for these two ru-grats we have. It has been a rollercoaster ride of excitement since I left the Pinas with Carl. I've got the man of my dreams; we have two beautiful kids, and the financial stability to do the things we want to and to go to the places we dream of."

Intently listening to Jennifer's story, Kathrina grows more curious to learn about Jennifer's experience. She asks Jennifer, "Do you mind me asking: what is your immigration status, now?"

Jennifer responds, "Of course not. I got my green card as soon as we were married and my oath taking to be a US citizen was just two months ago. It was one of the first things we did back here in California. Carl made it a very special day for me. His whole family and his closest friends from the unit wore their uniforms at my celebration. I'll never forget my oath taking. I cried tears of joy."

Jennifer, now curious to hear about Kathrina's story says, "Enough about me. Tell me about you and David! This conversation is so surreal. I can't believe our dreams have come true and we are both here in the US."

Before Kathrina can get a word out of her mouth, Jennifer continues, "We need to do a road trip together, there are so many places outside of California that I want to see. Carl is planning a military leave around the kids' spring break, we can all go jump in an RV and drive across the country. First stop, the Grand Canyon!"

Though aspirational and exciting as all this sounds to Kathrina, her body shudders at the idea of being stopped by border patrol or at a state-line checkpoint. Siting in silence and thinking the call has dropped, Jennifer says, "Hello. Kathrina, are you still there?"

Kathrina, now speaking in a shy and demure tone, states, "Jennifer, I have something embarrassing to tell you. David and I have both overstayed our visitor visas. We both came to visit and fell in love with the lifestyle. We live with a very wealthy old man in Brentwood, helping him with all of his household chores and running errands for him. But, you want to know what is even more depressing? I think David is content with this lifestyle."

Jennifer cuts in, "Kathrina, I'm so sorry. Please don't feel embarrassed. There are many good people who might have followed the wrong path, but this country is honestly lucky to have you here. Just keep working towards fixing your status; that's the only way you can fully appreciate the opportunities that exist here in the US."

Kathrina, becoming teary eyed, thanks Jennifer for the words of encouragement and expresses interest in learning more about the military life. She asks Jennifer, "What is the best part about being married to a military man? What are the benefits?"

Jennifer responds with, "The benefits are awesome. I just have to contend with the fear of him going to war and the danger associated with his training exercises. We get either base housing or a housing allowance wherever Carl gets stationed. Medical, dental, and vision are covered by the military doctors. We get great medical care and we don't have to pay a penny, not even for medicine. On base we can purchase food, gasoline, and clothing without paying sales tax! There is a great support group among the non-serving military spouses. Childcare is not a problem and we have access to great education for the kids. Other than the fear of war and constant moving, if you don't like that, I can't think of anything someone wouldn't like about the benefits."

Kathrina asks, "What about Filipinos? Do you get homesick? Do you feel left out?"

Jennifer in response: "Absolutely not! There are so many Filipinos in the U.S. military. I get homesick, but even in France there was a Filipino community on the base. We had plenty of potlucks to share Filipino cuisine and I was able to meet people who will certainly be lifelong friends. In fact, our neighbors in France were Filipino – a cute lesbian couple. They have a couple of kids who played with ours. We'd help each other by babysitting on date nights."

Surprised Kathrina interrupts, "Wait did you say lesbians? That's allowed?"

Jennifer explains, "Before 2011 homosexuals were able to serve under the 'don't ask, don't tell' pretense. But in 2011, Congress voted to lift the ban that didn't allow homosexuals to serve openly. So, our neighbors, Rona and Shirley, were not prohibited in any way to show their affections for each other. Rona actually worked in the same unit with Carl."

Kathrina, surprised: "I had no idea that the military had become so liberal. I always thought it was ultraconservative. You said they have kids?"

In a matter of fact tone Jennifer replies, "Yes, two boys and a girl. Shirley was married to a guy before she met Rona. She had all the kids with him. Shirley and her ex-husband were both in the military and stationed on the same base. They were only married for 3 years and by the end of Shirley's enlistment they decided to divorce. Her husband stayed in the military and I think he's still in France. He and Shirley agreed to send the kids back to the States to stay with their grandmother for a little while. Shirley spent a few months backpacking in Europe and met Rona at a hostel while she was on leave. They bonded quickly, and Shirley decided to stay in France with Rona. She sent for the kids about 6 months later at the end of their school semester. They have been one happy family since then."

Kathrina gasps, "Wow, talk about modern family!"

Jennifer affirms, "Yeah, Rona brings home the bacon and Shirley takes care of the house and the kids. Rona is very dominant. It's clear she wears the pants and calls the shots. Sometimes I feel she is more macho than Carl. When we are together, Rona sits with Carl talks about old boot camp stories and sports. Even Carl can't keep up with her knowledge of football and basketball news. I think Rona is trying a little too hard sometimes to over compensate for being a woman in what is traditionally considered a man's role. Rona is very jealous and obsessive about Shirley. If she sees a guy looking too hard or smiling too much, she's quick to mark her territory or to become confrontational. She is the primary source of income for the couple; Shirley doesn't even work a part-time job. She gets child support for the kids and does all the domestic duties."

Kathrina inquires, "Do you guys miss them? Sounds like you know them quite well."

Jennifer says, "Absolutely, but we might be reunited soon! Carl just told me yesterday that Rona is being transferred here and that they will be working in the same unit again." Kathrina, yawning states, "Oh my goodness, look at the time. I can't believe it is already nearly midnight. I am really enjoying this conversation, but we should get some rest."

Jennifer agrees: "Yes I need to recharge to deal with these kids in the morning. I'm so excited to be catching up with you. Please let's talk again soon. Have a good night."

Kathrina says, "Goodnight, bye Jennifer."

Kathrina hangs up the phone and reaches over to turn off the lamp on the bedside table. Just as she is closing her eyes to rest, David barges into the room and turns on the lights so that he can get ready for bed. Kathrina, with the pillow over her head to block the light, yells, "What have you been doing all night? Have you been playing that game the whole time since you got home?"

David pretends he doesn't hear Kathrina, grabs his pajamas, and walks into the bathroom to freshen up for bed. After a long day, Kathrina is exhausted and falls asleep before David comes back to bed. David, trying to be as considerate and gentle as possible, rolls into his space on the bed after turning out the lights. Although, the day has been long for him he still hasn't had his fill of video game entertainment. Rather than going to sleep, he decides to download a new game app onto his phone that one of his buddies was raving about during his Call of Duty session. He downloads the app and within minutes he's addicted! Seconds turn into minutes, minutes turn into hours and without conscious effort he has been playing the app for close to two hours. It's now 2:00 A.M. Kathrina rolls over and the bright light emanating from David's phone beams through her eyelids like a spot light. Kathrina jumps and yells at David, "Are you seriously still playing games? Do you realize how late it is?" David just ignores her and continues playing.

Kathrina wishfully states, "Why can't you apply the same type of motivation and effort to your responsibilities as the man of the house?"

David responds, "What are you talking about, I took out the trash!"

Kathrina, annoyed with his lack of attention: "Will you put that damn game down! I'm talking about the car payment, our phone bill, and the credit card payments. Did you take care of them?"

David giggles, "They will take care of themselves; I will pay them when I get to it."

Kathrina responds, "David I'm serious, don't you realize we will need to keep our credit in order if we ever plan to buy a house? What is your plan for our future?"

David states, "Future, who is thinking about that? We are still young. We don't have kids. We have what we need now. We have food, a place to sleep, transportation and money for recreational use."

Furious now, Kathrina slams her hands on the bed and says, "We are dependent on Mr. Bradshaw wanting to keep us around. What happens when he dies? He is an old man. You know I have Crohn's disease! Every time we go to the doctor we have to pay excessive fees because we don't have insurance! We need jobs that have benefits and offer some degree of consistency. Living check to check and being dependent on Mr. Bradshaw is a terrible risk! Not only are our lives at risk, but my family depends on the money I send back home for my niece to go to school and to my undocumented parents."

Kathrina exclaims, "Be a fucking man! Make a plan. You need to grow up and realize that life is more than just fun and games. We can't continue like this. We need a path to citizenship so that we can get real jobs. You need to care and help me figure this out."

Losing patience in Kathrina's late night nagging, David decides to get up and sleep on the couch. He snatches a blanket from the closet and slams the door as he exits. Kathrina is feeling a cyclone of emotions: anger, fear and sadness engulf her consciousness. At the center of the storm is her clear resolve to do whatever it takes to correct her path in life. Tears fill her eyes as she stares into the dark ceiling and closes her eyes to sleep.

Chapter 4: Life with Mr. Bradshaw

Deep in sleep, David and Kathrina's snoring build a rhythmic alberti bass composition of sound and vibrations. The snoring reaches a crescendo of cacophony as the ringtone on David's mobile phone contributes a high-pitched, fast moving melody that eventually takes full stage. David and Kathrina are jarred awake as a disoriented David fumbles to find his phone on the bedside table. He answers with a cracking voice, "Hello?" On the other end of the line, "David, this is Mr. Bradshaw. I need you to get the car ready. I'm not feeling well. I have a slight fever and I think I might be coming down with a virus. I want to go to urgent care!"

After a deliberate pause in hopes that he is dreaming, David responds, "Ok, Mr. Bradshaw we will be right over!"

Upon ending the call, a furious Kathrina shrieks, "Its fucking 4:00 A.M. What is he thinking? Why is he even up?!" Already out of bed and grabbing his pants to get ready, David just sighs. Kathrina continues, "You know we aren't slaves. Just because he says 'jump' we shouldn't have to. Mr. Bradshaw does this to us all the time. He spends too much time on Google; anytime he has a small cough or the slightest fever he thinks he has ebola virus or something. He's a freaking cyberchondriac; I bet you he didn't sleep last night. He just sat at his desk googling symptoms."

David now growing annoyed with Kathrina's nagging and pessimism, "Come on, you know the routine. You need to get over there and prepare his clothes and breakfast so that we can get on with the day! You want the bills paid, right?" David grabs the keys and goes to check on the car. Realizing he forgot to fill up the tank the day prior, he sends Mr. Bradshaw a text letting him know that he will run to the gas station and be back in 30 minutes. Meanwhile, Kathrina throws on some gym clothes and puts her hair in a bun so that she can rush over to assist Mr. Bradshaw. As soon as she walks in the door, Mr. Bradshaw is already siting in the kitchen nook sipping on a hot cup of coffee. He exclaims, "Why the fuck am I always waiting on your guys? I pay you good money to be at my side. I don't understand how you guys can't appreciate the opportunities that you have because of me! I'm not feeling well and you take your sweet time."

Kathrina replies in a demure and submissive tone, "I'm so sorry Mr. Bradshaw; we do appreciate you and we will try harder to ensure that we can better anticipate your needs. Would you like me to prepare you a quick breakfast before I iron your shirt?" In a kinder tone, Mr. Bradshaw states, "Just some eggs and a warm croissant." Moving with a sense of urgency to satisfy their benefactor, Kathrina starts preparing his meal while he quietly drinks his coffee and watches the early Fox News report. Overwhelmed with brewing frustrations, Kathrina must bite her tongue, but physically she is tense and can't help but to imagine that as she is cracking his eggs she is actually cracking Mr. Bradshaw's skull; she further releases her physical tension by thoroughly beating his eggs. Like a tenured quick order chef, she serves up his breakfast and moves on to begin preparing his clothes. Reaching into his bedroom closet she is repulsed by the breath-stealing odor of mothballs and old shoes. She selects a simple blue oxford shirt and khaki pants for Mr. Bradshaw.

Mr. Bradshaw finishes his meal and is now pacing the floor in the hallway outside of the laundry room. He exclaims, "Aren't you done yet? Where is David? He should be back by now." Kathrina hands Mr. Bradshaw a hanger with his crisply ironed shirt and pants and he retires to the master bedroom to get dressed.

Kathrina takes a deep breath and sits on the living room couch to rest and recover from Mr. Bradshaw's pestering insistence. She turns on the TV in hopes of finding a quick escape and with the volume muted, flips through the channels stopping on the Travel Channel. She is entranced by beautiful images of the landscapes that make up the Grand Canyon. She can't hear the travel advisor's commentary, but the images are enough to transport her to the wonders that the Canyon hold: white water rafting down the Colorado river, zip lining across the canyon, backpacking into and camping on the floor of the Canyon. She imagines the trip capped off by sipping wine and eating artisan cheeses from the hotel balcony overlooking the Canyon. She can almost taste the cheese and wine, when David bursts through the front door in a flurry worried about Mr. Bradshaw's dwindling patience. Though early in the morning, Kathrina looks up from the TV with a face that reads exhaustion. David inquires, "Is he ready? The tank is full, and the car is out front."

Kathrina responds, "I'm not sure, why don't you go check? I can't take anymore right now."

David solemnly begins his walks toward the stairway to go up and check on Mr. Bradshaw when he appears at the top of the stairs. A frowning Mr. Bradshaw states, "Well what are you waiting for? Why don't you come up and give me a hand." With a "Yes sir," David obliges and proceeds to assist Mr. Bradshaw down the stairs and out to the car. Mr. Bradshaw pauses on the way out of the door and gives orders to Kathrina, "I have an eleven o'clock meeting with a publishing assistant to go over the contract on my next book. Could you make sure the place is presentable and I'd like you to prepare some freshly baked cookies and tea."

Kathrina affirms, "Will do Mr. Bradshaw."

Each day serving Mr. Bradshaw is a constant drain on Kathrina and David's patience and sanity. Each day is a repeat of the previous: dealing with an ever increasingly angry, grumpy, impatient, and unappreciative old man. He knows that he has leverage over them and can essentially treat them like indentured servants because of their immigration status. He constantly berates them and pushes the limits of what is reasonable and acceptable of an employer.

Mr. Bradshaw is a widower with three kids who never find the time to come visit him. David and Kathrina began caring for him about six years ago when Mr. Bradshaw's wife passed away. Kathrina has speculated that depression and loneliness are the source of his behavior and initially was able to ignore and tolerate how he treats them. Outside of holidays, not even his children are willing to tolerate his emotional issues.

Kathrina was introduced to Mr. Bradshaw by her Tita Eileen's friend, Caroline, who worked as an RN at the hospital that treated Mrs. Bradshaw prior to her passing. Caroline, like most nurses, has an extremely kind heart and could see that Mr. Bradshaw was going to need a caretaker in order to comfortably continue living alone. Knowing that Kathrina was struggling to find work, she immediately jumped at the opportunity to connect the two. Kathrina quickly became a fixture in Mr. Bradshaw's life. After only a few months of working for him, she moved into the pool house on his property so that she could better attend to his needs. This proved to be an ideal opportunity for her because despite the low pay, he provided her with a place to stay so that she didn't have to depend on friends and family. This newfound freedom allowed Kathrina the flexibility to dream big and to get a taste of what it is to live the American dream. She had been dating David for quite some time when she started working for Mr. Bradshaw. He was working under the table doing odd jobs for his uncle, who is a general contractor specializing in computer network infrastructure and design. David would come in on the large projects to help install cabling for computer servers and voice communications systems. Mr. Bradshaw's failing eyesight made it very difficult for him to drive and Kathrina never felt comfortable driving. So, she made a proposal to Mr. Bradshaw one day while he was driving to the market with Kathrina for groceries. She explained to Mr. Bradshaw that her boyfriend could bring value to their arrangement by providing driving services, assisting him with his technological needs at the house as a writer and by doing all the heavy lifting and overseeing care of his estate. This opportunity would give David a more stable form of work and allow her and David to spend more time together in their budding relationship. Mr. Bradshaw would, inturn, receive the dedicated care of an on-call domestic couple. He agreed to allow David to move in with Kathrina and increased his monthly commitment to her from $1,500 to $2,500, with David starting immediately. In his downtime, David would still continue to help his uncle for additional income, whenever Mr. Bradshaw wasn't demanding attention.

Mr. Bradshaw worked many years as a freelance writer for conservative newspapers. In his lifetime he covered subjects involving the civil rights movement, abortion, gay rights, immigration, and the economy. His views and opinions have always been extremely, "right" and despite his position on restrictive immigration, he is essentially supporting an illegal immigrant couple. It's almost as if he is making up for the guilt of contradicting his principles by tormenting the couple with every opportunity he gets. After 30 years as a writer, Mr. Bradshaw moved into an editorial role with the *Wall Street Chronicles*, where he worked hard to fast track articles that helped to support a restrictive approach to immigration. He battled policies presented by liberals that called for social welfare toward immigrants who entered the US illegally, especially those from third-world countries whom he believed were not only stealing American jobs but also tainting American culture and morals. He had a higher tolerance toward some groups, but his efforts to fight the trend of immigration were firm and unwavering. Mr. Bradshaw censored the efforts of progressive writing conservatives who focused on the plight of African Americans from slavery to mass incarceration. Inclusion and equality to him were a waste of time and the American society's resources. It was his belief that African Americans had just as much opportunity as anyone else to be successful in this country and that it is the responsibility of those communities to make positive changes on their own accord.

Around the time of Barrack Obama's campaign and under the pressure of the budding rise of millennials, the WSC started moving in a more progressive direction. The overtly ultra-conservative views that he perpetuated were losing ground and popularity. They realized that the aging Baby Boomers wouldn't be enough to sustain sales without the attention of the millennials. So, Mr. Bradshaw was asked to step down as the lead editor to allow for a younger editor with slightly more progressive views. Given that his wife was already battling breast cancer, he happily obliged and entered into retirement. Retirement got old very fast for Mr. Bradshaw and it didn't take long for him to start writing historical pieces detailing his experiences and conservative positions in retrospect to what had occurred. He hoped to inspire a newfound movement toward ultra-conservative views. Poor David was subject to taking dictation and typing out much of this propaganda in the evenings before Mr. Bradshaw would have dinner.

By Friday morning, David and Kathrina are a little more exhausted than usual as Mr. Bradshaw seems to be getting harder and harder to please and to tolerate with each day. Still in bed, Kathrina rolls over and in a surprised tone comments to David, "Wow its already 8:00 A.M. and not a peep from Mr. Bradshaw! This is eerie; maybe he's dead?"

A complicit David responds, "We couldn't be so lucky!"

Kathrina now feeling guilty, "Let's not be so morbid and evil. All jokes aside, Mr. Bradshaw is getting old. We need a plan for our future."

David agrees and comments in a suggestive manner, "I think we need a vacation! How about we connect with your friend Jennifer? She seems cool. Why don't you see what she is doing this weekend. Maybe we can go on a road trip to the Grand Canyon." With exuberance and renewed vigor, Kathrina responds with a resoundingly simple but firm, "Ok!"

Chapter 5: The Getaway

Peeking around the corner and into Mr. Bradshaw's study, Kathrina inquires, "Good afternoon Mr. Bradshaw, I was planning to prepare spaghetti for your lunch today. Would you like red or white wine served with it?" A grumpy as usual Bradshaw responds, "Surprise me!" Kathrina walks to the kitchen and in her mind plans the steps for preparing Mr. Bradshaw's meal. She gathers all the ingredients for the sauce – tomato paste, crushed tomatoes, garlic, basil, mushrooms and onion. She is on autopilot chopping up the veggies and throwing everything into the sauce pan. Then she cuts and butters a piece of bread with garlic butter to go in the toaster. Nearly halfway through the day, she so excited about the opportunity to get away from it all that she's having flashbacks to the images she saw of the Grand Canyon. While the sauce simmers she decides to check in with Jennifer to see if she and Carl are up for a spontaneous trip to the Grand Canyon. With onion-and-garlic-infused hands, she reaches for her phone without a care and places the call. Answering on the first ring, an excited Jennifer says, "Hey girl! What's up? How are you?"

Kathrina responds, "Just the usual, here caring for Mr. Bradshaw. How are you doing?"

Jennifer says, "Oh I'm just trying to survive motherhood! These kids are a handful. Keeping up with their studies, their extracurricular activities and the housework; motherhood being a fulltime job is an understatement."

Kathrina quickly interjects and whispers, "I'll trade you a Brady Bunch of kids for this guy over here." An eruption of laughter ensues, and Mr. Bradshaw yells out, "Kathrina I'm trying to work in here!" Her laughter recedes to the equivalent of a teenage girl's giggling. Joking with Jennifer, Kathrina says, "Uh oh, I'm in trouble with the principal." After getting a good laugh out, Kathrina makes a proposal, "Jennifer, sounds like we both need a break. How about you and Carl join us for a trip? I know it's last minute, but let's do it….Please?"

An excited Jennifer responds, "That's actually a really good idea. Let me talk to Carl. I'll call you back in a little while."

Kathrina is so distracted and in a different world she has forgotten to cook the pasta. She exclaims, "Tang ina!!!" Mr. Bradshaw emerges, practically charging into the kitchen as if the chow time bell has rung, adding hunger to his persona is a mad mix. Mr. Bradshaw hangrily inquires, "Where's my lunch?"

Quick on her toes, Kathrina prepares a salad as a distraction while the pasta boils and serves it to Mr. Bradshaw. Already knowing that Bradshaw could care less about a salad, she's hoping he's hungry enough to accept it.

Taking the salad from her he asks, "What is this? I thought you were serving me spaghetti. Why are you presenting me with rabbit food?"

With a huge smile, Kathrina responds, "Doctor's orders, Mr. Bradshaw. You need more fiber in your diet for digestive health." Grumbling incoherently, Mr. Bradshaw accepts the offering and scowls at Kathrina while chewing the greens. Mission accomplished, Kathrina serves the al dente pasta to Mr. Bradshaw and "Mr. Hyde" morphs back into a manageable "Dr. Jekyll." Smiling huge, a piece of lettuce covers his front teeth as he says, "Thank you, Kathrina."

Kathrina, holding back what feels like a deluge of laughter coming up from her tummy, releases just a giggle and responds, "You are very welcome, sir."

Kathrina is in a good mood while cleaning up after lunch and she has upbeat music quietly playing on her phone while she dances around the kitchen and lip syncs along. Mr. Bradshaw is in the middle of his afternoon nap. The music cuts out and initially she thinks her phone has died, but realizes she has an incoming call. She rushes over to check her phone and it's Jennifer. With enthusiasm she answers, "Hi Jennifer, what's the verdict?" There's a pause while Kathrina's heart sinks.

Jennifer responding almost lifelessly, "Sorry, we can't go . . . Naw, I'm just kidding girl! Carl is super excited too. We will leave the kids with his mom."

Relieved, Kathrina responds, "You got me! In honesty, we don't have an itinerary set yet. We just know that we want to go to the Grand Canyon. Is that ok?" Jennifer says, "Absolutely, just sleeping in another bed away from these kids is going to be so relaxing! We are open to spontaneity. What time did you want to leave?"

Kathrina says, "Pack your stuff and let's plan to get out of dodge by 6:00 A.M. tomorrow morning!"

Jennifer says, "Sounds like a plan. We will be ready. I will text you our address."

Waking from his nap, Mr. Bradshaw calls out, "Kathrina where's David? I don't feel like typing. Please be a doll and ask David to come take dictation for me."

Just sitting down to rest after cleaning and preparing meals for Mr. Bradshaw through the night and the weekend, Kathrina responds, "Yes sir!" Physically drained and fatigued, Kathrina must rock back and forth to gain the momentum to rise from the cushy sofa. She hits the redial and David answers, "Hello ganda?"

Kathrina smiling, "His majesty, beckons! He wants you to come take dictation."

"Ok, I'm nearly done washing the car; tell him I'll be right there," says David. When David enters the house, Kathrina pulls him aside because they need to work out a plan of attack to present their weekend plans to Mr. Bradshaw. Walking into Mr. Bradshaw's study together, they hold hands as if they are going to meet the great and powerful Wizard of Oz. David is a combination of the scarecrow without a brain, the lion without courage, and the tin man without a heart to love and Kathrina is trying to find her way to Kansas to live out her American Dream.

Just as Dorothy had mighty courage, she speaks first: "Mr. Bradshaw, we appreciate all that you have done for us. We do our best to meet and anticipate your needs. David and I would like to take off a couple of days this weekend."

Mr. Bradshaw grumbles, "Just make sure I have food to get through the weekend. I don't want to cook!"

A nervous David responds, "Thank you so much, Mr. Bradshaw."

David finishes taking dictation and hurries back to the guest house where he finds Kathrina packing. He grabs his favorite jeans, a couple of shirts, underclothes, and his toiletries and stuffs them in a backpack. Kathrina with a disgusted look says, "Are those even clean? You should fold your clothes before you put them in the bag. Please don't embarrass me in front of Jennifer and Carl." David scoffs, "I thought we were going to get away and relax. Do I need a getaway from you? Kulmalma KA! Stop nagging!"

In bed the couple is as giddy as two kids on the night before Christmas. They joke and reminisce about the week. They are all smiles as if a great weight has been lifted off of their shoulders. For once in a long time, they feel like a couple and exchange innocent soft kisses. Cuddling tightly, Kathrina rests her head on David's chest and falls asleep to the soothing rhythmic vibrations of his snoring.

The next morning Kathrina awakens to the fragrance of fresh coffee and a kiss on her forehead from David. Pleasantly surprised, her eyes open wide and a smile paints her face. She drinks her coffee and joins David in the bathroom to get dressed for their road trip. While in the bathroom, Jennifer calls, "Good morning Kathrina! Are you ready to do this?"

With reciprocal exuberance, "Yes girl, let's get this show on the road. Will you text me your address? David and I will be heading over to your place in about thirty minutes."

On the way to pick up Jennifer and Carl, Kathrina realizes the address that she has provided them is on the Air Station. Having never visited a military base before, she looks over to David and inquires, "Babe, this address is on a military base. Do you think they will ask for credentials?

"Hay Naku! Don't they have security checkpoints?" David responds, "Relax we are just picking up friends. Did you tell Jennifer your status? If it were an issue, I'm sure she would have told you something." Arriving at the gate to the base, David kids around, "Ok put your game face on. We don't want to end up locked up at Guantanamo Bay and being water boarded."

"Shut up you idiot," an annoyed Kathrina responds. They pull forward to the sentry and he waves them through the checkpoint. They proceed to follow the directions to meet Jennifer and Carl at their place.

Now on their way to the Grand Canyon, Kathrina and David start to bond with Jennifer and Carl. Jennifer and Kathrina break the ice by sharing stories about their school days: stories about dating lame mama's boys, studying hard for exams, and their dreams of becoming US citizens. Carl contributes stories summarizing his experience in the military, his infatuation with Asian foods, and how lucky he feels he is to have met such a beautiful and loving woman in Jennifer. He feels lucky to have met a woman that truly loves him and he's blown away by her fascination with him. Finding love in the Philippines was never something that he anticipated happening. He brags about the beautiful children that they have had together and how each of them have inherited specific physical and personality characteristics that he loves about her.

Kathrina acknowledges they are living the American Dream stating, "You guys are living the life. David and I are thinking to have kids, but there's too much risk for us at this time."

David chimes in with, "Hey Carl. Being a military man, you have to appreciate 'Call of Duty,'" David is desperate to change the conversation. Before Carl can respond, Kathrina rebuts "David nobody cares about 'Call of Duty.' Ok!"

Almost halfway to the Grand Canyon, the couples decide to stop for brunch. Carl spots a sign for the Golden Corral and they exit the highway near the California border to eat. Having never eaten at this place, the multitude of options available at the buffet sounds like a great plan. Carl and David go through the line first and load their plates with practically one of everything. Carl has flashbacks to his boot camp days and kids about David taking too long to progress through the line. As David fumbles with the scrambled eggs, Carl shouts, "One shot, One kill recruit . . . Keep it moving!" The couples sit and begin to dig into their meals when Jennifer receives a call. Nonchalantly, she checks the caller id and places her attention back on her meal and present company. As soon as she places the next spoonful in her mouth the phone begins ringing again, this time out loud, "Hay Naku! What could be so important?" Politely asking to be excused from the table, Jennifer walks away and answers the call, "Hello Rona. What's up?"

A sobbing Rona responds, "Jennifer I'm sorry to bug you. I just needed someone to talk to."

Jennifer, growing concerned in reaction to the distress in Rona's voice inquires, "What's wrong honey? What happened?" Rona calming only slightly now that she has Jennifer's attention responds, "Jennifer, I think this bitch is cheating on me with one of her ex-husband's friends? This guy was transferred here last week, and she couldn't wait to invite him over for dinner. They say they haven't seen each other in years, but it seems to me like they been talking all along. Even the kids know and like him!"

Jennifer, thinking that Rona is just being jealous and paranoid replies, "Rona seriously! You have to be more confident. When does Shirley even have time to cheat? You are not being reasonable or rational about this. Just calm down and spend some time getting to know the guy. Don't jump to conclusions." Giggling, she says, "Maybe you should give her a little to worry about, why don't you join us on our little getaway?"

Rona responds, "Where are you?" Jennifer says, "We are halfway to the Grand Canyon! Come treat yourself and get away from Shirley and her pesky kids for the weekend." The line goes silent and then Rona responds, "That is so tempting! How will I get there?" Jennifer suggests, "Carl did some research before we decided to drive out with our friends and he found out that Amtrak has a stop in Williams, AZ. We will stop and sleep there tonight before we move into the National Park tomorrow morning. You should catch the train and meet us there. We rented an AirBnb and with three bedrooms, so there is plenty of space."

"Fuck it, I'm online already and booking my ticket. Looks like I'll arrive around 9 P.M. if I catch the train around 1 P.M. Will you guys still be up?

Jennifer responds, "Hell yeah. We are turning the clock back to 1995. There will be no sleeping. We will party until we drop."

An unimpressed Rona replies, "Yeah right, I've seen you drink! Two glasses of wine and you are already in lala land. Don't leave me stranded at the train station, ok? I'm going to get packed and head over to the train station."

Jennifer returns to the breakfast table with a huge smile on her face. Everyone is curious to know what transpired on her phone call. She explains that their friend Rona will be joining the party and shouts, "The more the merrier, right?" Carl raises his orange juice and proposes a symbolic toast, "To friends new and old. To adventures undisclosed. Let's get this party back on the road!"

Everyone breaks into laughter and immediately focuses on getting their morning fill so that they can resume their travels.

Back on the road and noticing the sign that says "Arizona 10 miles," Kathrina begins to feel anxious. She looks over at David and he's knocked out. The snoring coming from the backseat is almost loud enough to drown out the soft rock playing over the radio. In her mind, Kathrina has images of being questioned and detained by the border patrol agents. She imagines being locked up and being treated like an animal, having to shower among strange women and eat terrible food while dressed in orange jumpsuits. The anxiety becomes overwhelming and she decides to pull off the freeway at that nearest rest area.

As she is pulling into the parking lot, the low hum and vibration of the ride recedes, and everyone awakens like baby who loses his pacifier. Disoriented, rubbing eyes and stretching, they all wonder what is going on. Finally, David inquires, "Where are we honey?"

Kathrina afraid to admit she is anxious and afraid about the border crossing, replies, "Oh I've got to make a pit stop to use the restroom. Anyone else? Jennifer, will you please come with me? Rest areas are spooky to me."

Reaching for her shoes, Jennifer obliges, and they walk over to the restroom with wobbly legs from sitting in the car for so long. At the sink, Jennifer notices that Kathrina's hands are shaking uncontrollably.

She inquires, "What's wrong sweetheart?"

In a trembling voice, Kathrina responds, "I'm embarrassed to say that I am really worried about the border checkpoint. I know it's probably no big deal, but being deported is my biggest nightmare."

Jennifer responds, "It all good. Relax Kathrina, I'll suggest that Carl and I take the pilot and co-pilot responsibilities when we get back to the car. We will chauffer you guys across the border. If we get stopped, Carl will show his military ID or they will see his military tattoos and then I'm sure the agent will wave us through without any questions."

Feeling relieved, Kathrina hugs Jennifer tightly and hands her the keys.

At the border checkpoint, Carl is driving and there is only one agent manning a single lane of traffic. As the car approaches the checkpoint, the agent takes a quick look through the windshield and waves them through. Only four hours from their destination, the group is reinvigorated with excitement as Carl bumps the Black Eyed Peas playlist from his phone over the car's Bluetooth connection. The couples are getting "retarded" as the Black Eyed Peas song implies, bobbing their heads and singing along.

Suddenly, David yells, "Turn it down, turn it down!" Jennifer reaches and turns the radio down and then David answers his phone, "Hello Mr. Bradshaw."

Mr. Bradshaw answers speaking loudly, "DAVID! DAVID! Are you there?" David presses the phone tightly against his ear, embarrassed that Carl or Jennifer might hear the drama. David responding, "Hello Mr. Bradshaw, I'm here. Are you ok?"

Mr. Bradshaw is speaking so loudly that his voice carries right through David's head and everyone is listening and giggling. Grumpy Bradshaw replies, "Speak up boy, so I can hear you!"

David, "Yes Mr. Bradshaw, I am here! What do you need?"

Mr. Bradshaw responds, "I need to know where your wife put the TV remote. I've been looking everywhere! The TV is on the stupid travel channel. I need to watch the Hannity report."

Before David can ask, Kathrina, says, "Tell him the remote is on the fireplace mantel next to flower vase." Afterwards, Kathrina and David spend time explaining the special intricacies of their relationship with Mr. Bradshaw as a result of their immigration status. They are both grateful to have an opportunity to earn money, but are demoralized by how Mr. Bradshaw treats them. There is a continuous struggle to bite their tongues so that they do not tell Mr. Bradshaw how they truly feel about him. Riding the front seat still, Carl and Jennifer just turn up the radio and encourage Kathrina and David that better days are ahead. The "roadtripalloza" continues and as the sun is setting they are already exiting the freeway into Williams, Arizona.

The couples check into the suite; they decide to order pizza for dinner and Carl and David step out to make a beer run. Kathrina and Jennifer place the pizza order and start going through the travel brochures from the hotel lobby. With wide eyes and a huge grin, Kathrina says, "You want to try the zip line across the canyon?"

Jennifer acts unfazed by the proposition, responding with "Zip line, that's child's play. If you want to get the adrenaline pumping, let's do the bungee jump!"

Both knowing how incredibly scared they are of high places, they erupt into laughter.

Kathrina says, "Let's think realistically! We will start at the visitor's center on the north rim."

Still window shopping Grand Canyon destinations by flipping through the images in the brochures, Jennifer replies, "Hey let's not settle for basic so quickly. We need some excitement in our lives."

Jennifer's phone begins to ring and without looking at the caller id, she assumes it's Carl calling from the grocery store. "Hey baby. What's up?"

On the other end of the call Rona jokes, "Hey baby, will you come pick me up?"

Jennifer laughs out loud, "Oh, Sorry Rona. I've lost track of time. I didn't expect you to be calling so soon. The guys are making a beer run at the grocery store and we just ordered pizza. I will tell them to swing around and pick you."

Rona says, "Awesome! Please tell them to get me some Stella Rosa Moscato."

Back at the hotel suite, the couples and Rona have enjoyed eating their pizza and are feeling the buzz from the beer and wine. It's a chilly evening and they are all sitting in the living room around the fireplace joking about their efforts to get away. David and Kathrina have escaped the plantation, Carl and Jennifer have escaped the preschool mad house, and Rona has escaped the anxiety of Shirley potentially cheating on her.

Kathrina asks a question of the group, "If you were home right now, what would you be doing?"

Jennifer the first to chime in, "I'd be rounding up my monkeys to get them in the bath. It's a chore just to get them in the water. Once they get wet, they turn into gremlins and there's more splashing in our bathroom than at an orca show at Sea World."

Kathrina quick to jump in, "So you have to clean up a little water? Try satisfying a grumpy, lonely old man who detests your existence in his country. We work our asses off for that man. He's getting old and as morbid as this sounds, I need him to live until the day I can tell him I have legal status and I quit!"

Rona patiently waiting to plead her case, "At least you guys have each other. My other half is good for nothing. I go to work then I have to come home to cook, clean, and care for her kids. I guess that's what I get for trying to grab eye candy. Then to top it off, she's probably the biggest flirt in the world."

Rona, singing the classic Coaster's song "Get an Ugly Girl to Marry You," "If you wanna be happy for the rest of your life, never make a pretty woman your wife. So, from my personal point of view get an ugly girl to marry you!" An eruption of hysterical laughter fills the room followed by an infectious yawn. Carl speaks out, "We better get some sleep. We have adventures ahead tomorrow. I was able to book us a private guide who is going to meet us at the visitor's center and take us down the base of the canyon. He said we should come well rested because it's not an easy task." All in agreement, they prepare for bed.

The next morning, everyone is awake at the break of dawn excited to start their adventure into the canyon. Making their way out of the small town of Williams, Arizona, they realize that they need to get fuel, not only for the car, but for themselves. After filling of the car, they head over to one of the local diners for a country breakfast feast on pancakes, French toast, bacon, hash browns, unlimited refills on coffee and to top it off they finish a whole apple pie à la mode!

At the entrance to the park, Kathrina is driving as they approach the ranger station. Her hands sweating and her heart racing with baseless anxiety, she greets the park ranger, "Good morning sir!"

The park ranger responds, "Welcome! What brings you to the park this morning?"

Kathrina, beginning to respond stutters, "Uh uh, we we."

Calmly David leans over and says, "We are here to hike down to the base of the canyon." The ranger inquires, "Do you have a guide? That's a very impressive feat. Hiking the canyon can be dangerous if you are a novice hiker."

From the backseat Carl responds, "Yes sir. We are meeting a guide from Happy Trails Tours. We are going on a hybrid hike, part on mule, part on foot."

The ranger replies, "You guys are in good hands. Drink lots of water and don't take chances! Here are some maps and the weather report. Enjoy your stay."

Arriving at the rim, the group is mesmerized by the beauty, the depth, the colors, and the magnificence of the Grand Canyon. No picture, no video, no words can match the experience or perspective of seeing the canyon with your own two eyes. For some, the canyon can invoke a sense of romance: Carl and Jennifer wander off to take selfies, kissing with the wondrous canyon as their background. Some realizing they are now among a select group of people to experience the canyon become vain: David becomes consumed with posting selfies and live videos on social media. The likes and the comments from his friends and followers feed his ego and validate his existence. For others, the grand depths and size of the canyon can inspire feelings of insignificance and loneliness. Kathrina and Rona stand near the rim of the canyon staring into the rocky abyss. In that moment, they simultaneously and unknowingly share a moment of romantic introspection.

In the distance Carl is yelling, "Hey we are going to be late. Come on let's go!" Looking up Kathrina and Rona can't help but notice the tears in each other's eyes. They simply smile and jog over to quickly catch up with their group so that they can make it to their appointment with the guide.

Later while descending into the canyon, the guide stops the group and asks everyone to dismount their mules. They have reached roughly the midpoint in the trek into the canyon and this portion of the trial will require them to hike on foot. David hurries off to the front of the caravan so that he can capture GoPro videos of himself leading everyone into the canyon. Jennifer is getting tired, so she's walking behind Carl with her hands on his shoulders as a support. Lagging behind the guide and struggling to keep up, Kathrina stumbles and falls. David, far ahead of the group, is too far to assist. The guide has his hands full with the mules and doesn't notice she has fallen. Carl is focused on getting Jennifer down to the bottom. The only person free to come to her aid is Rona. Rona inquires while extending a hand to assist, "Are you ok?"

Kathrina replies with blushing cheeks and reaches for Rona's hand, "Yes, thank you Rona. Just my ego is bruised." For the remainder of the hike into the canyon Rona walks by Kathrina's side continuously asking if she's ok and assisting her up and down the rugged terrain. Kathrina is full of smiles having

Rona's attention. Rona is feeling chivalrous like a knight in shining armor. The seeds of a new friendship begin to take root.

Chapter 6: Text Affair

On the way home and making the first stop at Rona's place, everyone is sad that their getaway has come to an end. Everyone says goodbye to Rona. She jumps out of the car and makes a quick stop at the passenger side window to speak to Kathrina. She looks past Kathrina towards David and says, "It was a pleasure meeting you guys. I'm so glad I had the opportunity to share this trip with you."

Now focusing on Kathrina, she says, "I'd really like to stay in touch with you guys. Would you please take my number? Call me anytime you want to talk about anything?"

Without hesitation, Kathrina exchanges numbers with Rona. Carl and Jennifer live a short distance from Rona on the same base. However, by the time they are dropping off the couple, everyone is either depressed to be returning to the daily grind on Monday or they are tired and looking forward jumping in bed. Kathrina expresses her gratitude to Carl and Jennifer for joining them and making the trip something to remember.

The next day it is business as usual. Kathrina is tending to Mr. Bradshaw's needs when she receives her first text from Rona. It's a simple, "Hi."

Kathrina smiles and thinks of something witty to respond with, "Uh who is this?"

Rona responds, "This is Rona. I'm sorry, who is this?"

Responding with a laughing out loud emoji, Kathrina, "It's me. I'm just messing with you. How are you?"

Rona is working the reception counter as an admin clerk and before she can respond a new airman is reporting for duty and presenting his orders to Rona. She sends a quick text back to Kathrina, "Sorry gotta run. I'm at work. Just wanted to say hi. TTYL."

Kathrina moves on to prepare Mr. Bradshaw's dinner. Having missed his caretakers, Mr. Bradshaw for once is full of *pleases* and *thank yous*. In fact, he invites the two of them to enjoy dinner with him. Kathrina and David for once feel appreciated and more like employees than indentured servants. After serving dinner, Kathrina is standing at the kitchen sink washing dishes. She receives another text from Rona, "Hey Kathrina it's me. How's it going?"

Kathrina grabs her phone with wet hands and responds, "Hey Rona. I'm just washing dishes after serving dinner."

Rona typing, "Sounds good, what did you eat?"

Kathrina responds, "I cooked Adobong Sitaw. Mr. Bradshaw likes Filipino dishes."

Rona, typing with her mouth watering, "OMG…I miss Filipino food. Shirley hates cooking. I get home late and then there's no time to spend cooking. I usually heat up something frozen like pasta from Trader Joes. I'm so jelly!"

Kathrina responds, "Where are you, let me finish cleaning up and I will text you later." Rona responds, "Sure give it a try. I might be driving Uber. If I don't respond, please don't think I don't want to talk."

Kathrina calls out to David from the living room couch, "Babe come watch Netflix with me. We have been back for almost two days and we haven't spent any time together."

David from his man cave, "Ok dear. Just ten more minutes!"

Kathrina, sitting on the couch alone with the show paused, jumps on social media to check her feeds. Scrolling through she sees all of the pictures posted by David and Jennifer from their Grand Canyon trip. She reminisces about the relaxation, fun and escape from the daily routine. She also can't help but notice that every one of Jennifer's posts are inclusive of Carl with some type of loving, appreciative caption while each of David's posts are of him doing something silly on his own to appease his followers. While liking one of Jennifer's posts she notices that Rona is Facebook friends with Jennifer. She's immediately compelled to request Rona's friendship. Almost instantaneously she receives confirmation that Rona has accepted her friendship and a spark of curiosity roars into flame of discovery. Kathrina checks for mutual friends, Rona's birthday, posted relationship status; she browses through the pics on her profile, and takes notice of Rona's likes and dislikes. Based on her post she makes the conclusion that Rona is very loyal and proud to serve her country. She's into fitness. She loves food. She's very vocal about LGBTQ rights and not ashamed of who she is. Her profile pictures are very family oriented: selfies are very rare. She has been snooping for 30 minutes and has totally lost track of time; as the TV shuts off and goes into sleep mode she is reminded that she'd asked David to join her. She yells out, "David where are you? I'm still waiting for you!" David doesn't respond. She knows that competing with his PlayStation is a battle that she will lose almost every time. Instead she turns on some music, pours a glass of wine, and cuddles up on the couch to relax and begins to doze off.

In a light, sleepy haze, she hears a couple of vibrations coming from the coffee table. Sitting up to check the notifications on her phone, her eyes open wide as she realizes it's Rona. There are two text messages: one from twenty minutes ago and another from seven minutes ago. In that moment she feels guilty for missing the messages and send a response, "Sorry I missed you, Rona. Are you still there?"

As soon as she hits send, she notices the message has been read and sees that Rona is responding. Her heart skips a beat in anticipation of Rona's response, "Hello Kathrina, I'm still here. I'm driving Uber and it's so slow tonight."

Kathrina responds, "I'm sorry. Maybe I'm bad luck accompanied by a (laughing and crying emoji)." Rona types back, "You aren't bad luck. I'm lucky to have met you. Are you stalking me on social media?" Wide awake, Kathrina replies, "No, I'm not stalking you. I'm getting to know you and adding more channels for you to reach out to me. Lol! We need to be in touch."

David, thinking that Kathrina is going to kill him, finally decides to get up and tiptoe over to the living room to spend time with her. R&B slow jams are playing in the background. He stands in front of her and begins lip syncing and grinding his hips to R Kelly's, "Bump N Grind." However, Kathrina is so enthralled in her witty text messaging volley with Rona that she doesn't notice him or his shadow. David decides to step his game up and begins to sing along with R Kelly. Completely out of tune and akin to the sound of clutch gears grinding, he sings, "I don't see nothing wroooong with a little bump and grind!"

Jumping out of her skin, Kathrina yells, "David! What the hell? You scared the shit out me. Why are you being silly?"

David responds, "Don't you miss me?"

Meanwhile she's missed a couple messages from Rona and Rona is beginning to wonder what's going. Rona tells her, "Let's catch up later, I've finally got a fare. Have a goodnight."

"Ok goodnight," replies Kathrina. Now dealing with David's sorry performance, she says "What's to miss about that? It's late let's just go to sleep."

At five o'clock in the morning Kathrina and David receive their friendly wake up call. It's Mr. Bradshaw, "David, did I tell you I have my senior golf tournament today? We need to be at the club for tee time at 6:30!" Before David can wake up to say a word, Mr. Bradshaw continues, "Load my clubs in the car and send Kathrina to make me breakfast." Without waiting for an acknowledgement or questions, Mr. Bradshaw ends the call.

For the first time in weeks, Carl isn't working in the field training new recruits and he decides to stop in on Rona. She's not paying attention and filling out paperwork when he walks up to the admin counter and says, "Tech Sergent Ware reporting for duty!"

Still not looking up Rona says, "Sorry, the officer on duty is out to lunch. Please wait in the lounge or come back around fourteen hundred."

With a sinister laugh, Carl says, "Rona it's me! I'm not in the field for once and thought you could use a lunch buddy. I've got steaks on my mind!"

Rona responds in a worrisome tone, "Wow Carl that sounds great, but I only have McDonald's money."

Slapping her on the shoulder, Carl states "Lunch is on me' let's go before I change my mind."

At lunch, Carl and Rona reminisce about their time serving together in France. They discuss all the fine dining, culture and tourism they were able to enjoy. Rona is very thankful for the tasty meal and explains to Carl how rare it is for her to enjoy fine meals anymore. She goes on to explain how she's working her ass off to keep her family together financially. He immediately makes an offer to lend them money, but Rona respectfully declines stating, "Carl, you and Jennifer have your own responsibilities! Don't worry about us. I'll make ends meet."

As she finishes her sentence she looks down and notices a message from Shirley. The messages reads: "Hey honey, sorry I missed your call. Meet you at the kids' practice tonight!" Carl sees the surprised look on her face and inquires if she's ok. Rona affirms that she's ok but insists that she has to leave quickly because the "officer on duty" is waiting for her. Carl thanks her for keeping him company at lunch and gives her hug.

Rona calls Shirley on her way back to the office, "Hey what was that message you sent me?"

Shirley stuttering and fumbling with her phone, "What message?"

Rona responds, "The one about meeting you at the kids practice. I told you I was going to drive Uber tonight. Who were you trying to text?"

Shirley responds, "Oh that message. No, I thought you were coming straight to practice to see the kids play."

Rona certain that Shirley is lying to her says, "You're a fucking liar," and hangs up the phone. Shirley calls back repeatedly, but Rona sends each call directly to voicemail.

Kissing Jennifer gently on the nose and holding her tight, Carl and Jennifer are cuddling on the couch after putting the kids to bed. He tells Jennifer about his lunch with Rona. He expresses concern about her financial situation, being overworked and the fact that he stills hears rumors among the guys that Shirley might be having an affair with his commanding officer, Captain Santos. He has been working under Captain Santos for about three years now and he's constantly bragging about some soccer mom that he's having an affair with. Captain Santos is a stud and has coached several of the base soccer teams to regional championships. He can't help but to wonder if Shirley is cheating on Rona with him after she has been working so hard to bring stability to her family. Carl and Jennifer are so upset by the matter that it interrupts their romantic moment, but then they come to realize how thankful they are for each other and continue snuggling and kissing.

In the morning after getting the kids ready for school, Jennifer gives Kathrina a call. They haven't spoken since coming back from the Grand Canyon. Kathrina is relaxing in Mr. Bradshaw's garden after serving him breakfast when she receives Jennifer's call, "Hey Jennifer, how are you?" says Kathrina.

Jennifer responds, "I'm just thinking about you. I miss you girl. How are you and David?"

Kathrina calmly states, "Oh just back to the same routine." She goes on to explain how much she is fed up with caring for Mr. Bradshaw and how she feels like she's spinning her wheels and not advancing much in life. Jennifer asks, "Well what do you think is holding you back? What do you need to do to fix this?"

Without hesitation Kathrina responds, "We need legal status!" Jennifer asks her what's their plan; Kathrina is completely dumbfounded and has no solutions. She explains that David has little to no ambition. As long as he has food and his PlayStation he's in heaven. If anything is to ever happen, she would have to be the one to champion change and progress. Kathrina explains how much she idolizes and envies the life that Jennifer has with Carl. She explains that she perceives Jennifer and Carl to be living the American Dream with a full pursuit of happiness and opportunity.

Jennifer comforts Kathrina and tells her, "We have shared dreams together since middle school. After all these years, I'm still by your side Kathrina. I promise I'll do whatever I can do to help."

Hearing grumbling from Mr. Bradshaw through the backdoor, Kathrina tells Jennifer, "Hey I've got to go. Thanks for being a true friend. I really appreciate it."

Later that evening, Kathrina is home alone watching crime shows on the Discovery Channel while David is out playing basketball with his friends. She's watching a special week-long series covering love affairs and crimes of passion. She is intrigued by the extents to which people go to find happiness in romance; she's amazed by how jealousy can fuel fits of extreme anger and frightened by how romantic passion can go deathly wrong. She's so fixated on her TV that she hasn't noticed that she has a couple of missed calls and text messages from Jennifer and Rona. Since Jennifer hasn't left a voicemail she decides to check Rona's text message first and then call Jennifer back. Rona's text message is short and to the point, "Hey miss you. How was your day?"

Kathrina responds, "Hi Rona, nothing special. How are you doing?"

After a while there is no response, so Kathrina goes back to watching her show, then during the commercial break Rona responds, "Sorry I was driving Uber, taking a dinner break now. I'm tired, but I've got bills to pay."

Kathrina inquires, "What are you eating?"

Rona replies, "Just some fake Mexican food from Taco Jack."

Kathrina sends a laughing out loud emoji and responds, "Mexican food is one of my specialties. I really enjoy making ceviche tostadas and shrimp cocktail."

Rona responds, "I'm so hungry right now I'd settle for cardboard. I wish I could come home to meal like that just once in a week!"

Feeling pity for Rona, but also proud of her commitment to home cooked meals, Kathrina replies, "If David wasn't so active playing basketball, he would probably be obese. I love cooking for him and I always have at least one cooked meal at the house ready to go."

Rona replies, "I could only dream of being so lucky!" Kathrina suggests, "if you are driving Uber tomorrow night, why don't you pick up Jennifer and come over for dinner? We can make it a lady's night. You bring wine, I'll cook, and Jennifer can pick a movie for us to watch."

Rona replies, "That sounds awesome. Hey, I've got another fare. Talk to you later, ok?"

Eager to showcase her cooking skills and spend time with the girls, Kathrina returns Jennifer's call, "Hey girlfriend!"

Jennifer responds, "Hi Kathrina, I was calling you earlier."

Kathrina explains she was distracted watching her crime shows and gives her the quick summary of her text exchange with Rona. She asks Jennifer if she can take some time off from her family and come have a lady's night. Jennifer speaks to Carl about it he's tells her to go for it; he knows that she's making an effort to help these two old friends be happy. Carl will stay home with the kids for some daddy bonding time. Jennifer accepts the invitation and speaks with Kathrina to arrange the pick-up time. After the phone call, Kathrina calls David and tells him he has to go bowling or something so that she can host a lady's night. David doesn't waste free passes; he calls a buddy before he gets back to the house from playing basketball and has his bowling night all planned out.

Kathrina, dressed in a floral sundress, is floating around as jolly as Cinderella lighting scented candles and setting the stage for her friends to come over. There's soft jazz to fill the background and dimmed ambient lighting near the dinner table. The meal is already prepared and presented in such a manner that it's looks like she's hosting royalty. The flatware is strategically placed and her finest wine glasses are on display. The fabric napkins and china with floral patterns almost compliment her sundress. Kathrina has prepared a full Mexican feast to showcase her skills and just as she begins to worry that everything is getting cold, the doorbell rings. She hurries over to answer the door where Rona and Jennifer greet her with hugs.

Rona, immediately noticing that Kathrina has gone above and beyond says, "Oh my god, I feel underdressed!" She hands Kathrina the wine and the ladies wash up to sit and eat.

After enjoying a wonderful meal, they sit to watch a romantic comedy. Kathrina pours each lady a glass of Moscato and dims the main lights for the feature presentation. Before hitting play, she prompts Jennifer and Rona to check in with their significant others so that the movie plays uninterrupted. Kathrina calls David and he is annoyed that he had to miss a frame of bowling because it's was too loud to take the call inside the alley. Carl is already in bed and sounds exhausted from having to care for the kids alone. Shirley doesn't answer. Rona calls repeatedly and sends texts, but there's no response. Rona tells Kathrina to start the movie, assuring her everything is ok. Halfway into the romantic comedy, the protagonist walks in on his wife having sex with the neighbor's young son. Kathrina and Jennifer begin laughing hysterically because the kid jumps up and runs out of the house completely naked. The husbands yells, "Wait, you forgot your happy meal!"

Rona has a contrary response to the scene; she asks to excuse herself to use the restroom. After waiting several minutes Jennifer decides to check on her. She finds Rona sitting on the toilet seat crying and it appears that she is texting someone. Perplexed, Jennifer asks, "Rona what's wrong? Why are you crying? What happened?"

Rona responds, "I'm so embarrassed! Please forgive me. It's just that the last scene from the movie made me think of Shirley. I came here to text her and she's not responding! It has been a really rough week for me. Bills are piling up and I'm worried that Shirley misses being with men! I'm trying my best, but it just seems like I always fall short."

Jennifer walks over to comfort Rona and tells her to take a deep breathe. She hugs her and convinces her to try to forget about her worries and enjoy the present company. Jennifer looses Rona's bun and says, "Come on! Let your hair down! I'll drive us back home, so you can drown some of these sorrows and appreciate the humor in the movie."

Smiling, Rona wipes the tears from her eyes, "You are right. Fuck this shit. Life is too short!" The three ladies laugh the night away.

Done with her morning chores, Kathrina is sitting on Mr. Bradshaw's patio enjoying some sun and sneaking in a mimosa while on duty. David is busy with Mr. Bradshaw taking dictation and Kathrina can hear their dialogue coming from the study. Mr. Bradshaw gives dictation for David to type and then asks that David read it back to him. However, with each line of dictation read back, it appears that Mr. Bradshaw is losing more and more patience tolerating David's accent. David reads back, "Illegal Immigrants stacking inventor-ie at the pac-tor-ie pelt it wasn't pair that they were paid low wages..."

Mr. Bradshaw loses it!

"What the hell are you saying? How long have you been here? Why can't you speak English like an American? Try it again, I don't know what you are saying!"

Though sympathetic to poor David, Kathrina's morning happy hour fuels an uncontrolled giggling session. While checking her social media feeds she sees that Arlene and her new boyfriend are getting very serious. Just as she is about to post a comment on one of their pictures she gets a new message notification. She clicks the notification bar and to her surprise it's Rona.

Rona's text reads, "Good morning. Hope you are doing well. Sorry about my dramatic moment the other night."

Kathrina responds, "We all have our moments; it's ok. I'm glad you were able to enjoy the rest of the night."

Rona replies, "Thanks for having us. I love your cooking. I hope I'm not interrupting your day."

Kathrina is flattered and says, "You're quickly becoming one of my favorite notifications. Please message me any time you feel like talking."

Rona says, "Are you sure? I can turn makulit in a hurry?"

Kathrina puts her worries of being annoying to rest by expressing her desires to get to know her better. She goes on to explain how hard it is to find friends as you get older. Life just gets really busy and nobody has time for anyone outside of their immediate circle. Sometimes it's good to have someone with whom you can escape your daily dramas. Rona ends the conversations letting Kathrina know that she has to return to work.

Jennifer has dropped off the kids at school and is on her way home when she decides to give Rona a call to check-in on how she's doing. Rona answers and is outside having a stress relieving smoke, "Hey Jennifer! Good morning."

Jennifer can hear the long drag between her name and the word good. She inquires, "Rona, Are you smoking? I thought you quit!"

Rona replies, "Oh my goodness, are you watching me?"

Jennifer responds, "I was calling to check on you. I wanted to know how you are feeling, but that fact that your smoking says a lot."

Rona, feeling very disgusted with herself, drops the smoke and stomps it out. She says, "Thanks for being a real friend Jennifer. You always look out for me. Thanks for cheering me up at Kathrina's house."

Jennifer assures her that she will always be by her side and that she really wants to see her happy. She poses a question to Rona, "What do you think it will take to make you happy? How do you get out of this rut and get your life back on track?"

Rona quickly responds, "Fifteen to twenty thousand dollars would be a great start! I feel like financial stability will remove so much stress and that it would allow me to spend more time at home with my family."

Jennifer responds, "I'm your friend and I promise you we are going to figure this out, ok? Don't give up. Just hang in there. Happiness is around the corner. Ok, I'm at the market now. Let me handle my chores and I'll catch up with you later. Stop smoking!"

Rona giggles and says, "Yes mom! Bye, talk to you later."

Jennifer is in bed and her eyes are fixated on the wall. Her thoughts drift in and out of focus from absolutely nothing to deep reflection on the challenges that her two close friends are facing. She's desperate to find a solution, but it seems so far out of reach. She takes a moment to sends a prayer up to God to thank Him for her many blessing. Carl jumps in bed next to her and waves his hand across her eyes because he's hungry for some attention. He inquires, "You find that wall more attractive than your tall, dark, and handsome husband?"

A smile cuts through the exhaustion and frustration on her face. She says, "Of course not baby! I love you Carl!" Jennifer goes on to explain the reasons for her aloof temperament and asks Carl to help. After hearing the facts: Rona is in debt and has no time to work on her relationship, Kathrina is trapped in her illegal immigrant status.

Carl stops Jennifer's discussion and says, "I have the perfect answer. It's right in front of your face baby!" Eager to hear what genius plan he has come up with she jumps out of bed and she has her hands on her hips, "What is it, what is it, tell me!" Carl calmly responds, "They should plan an arranged marriage. Rona gets money to pay her bills to focus on salvaging her relationship with Shirley and Kathrina or David gets legal status to be here and can apply for a real job. After a couple of years, they dissolve the marriage and everyone lives happily ever after! Problems solved."

Jennifer responds, "That's simple, but perfect. That's why I married you baby. You're are so intelligent, and I find that sexy. Come give me a kiss!"

Chapter 7: The Proposal

Rona is working the reception desk again when she receives a call from a bill collector threatening to take her car if she doesn't bring the payment current immediately. The collector proposes that she surrender the car if she cannot make the payments. She explains that the car allows her to earn extra income for her family and that she cannot afford to return the car. Pleading she asks the collector if there are any other solutions to her dilemma and provides assurances that she is working diligently to get her accounts in order. The agent, appearing to be empathetic to her attempts, agrees to work out a payment arrangement plan that would bring her current without losing the use of the vehicle. Rona profusely thanks the collector, knowing she has only put a band-aid on a bigger problem.

On her break, she calls Jennifer to vent about the exchange with the collector and how desperate she is to get her accounts in order. Her emotions well up and she begins to cry on the phone. Jennifer tries her best to calm her down, "Rona don't cry. Think about the positive things happening in your life."

Rona responds, "Why is life so damn unfair? I try to do what's right. I try to be the best person I can be. I chose to spend part of my life serving my country. I live my life by the golden rule: treat others the way you want to be treated. But at the end of the day, it feels like I'm always in an uphill battle."

Jennifer replies, "I hear you Rona, but you are not alone. Just hang in there and don't give up. Let's talk this evening. I think I might have a solution."

Still emotional, Rona thanks Jennifer for listening to her and promises her that she will call later in the evening to hear her solution.

Rona sends a text to Kathrina on her way back to the office from lunch, "Hello maganda. How are you?"

The iMessage typing icon pops up in the chat window and Rona's heart is racing waiting to see how Kathrina will reply.

Kathrina responds, "Maganda? You talking about me?" and follows the text with a blushing emoji.

Rona writes, "Is this Kathrina Mendoza?"

Kathrina types, "Yes."

Rona replies, "THEN YES! You are maganda!"

Accompanied by a laughing out loud emoji, Kathrina writes, "I think you need to see your eye doctor and get your prescription checked."

Rona replies, "All jokes aside, I'm thankful to you for being a part of my life. Going to cook dinner for Shirley and the kids. Any suggestions for a recipe?"

Kathrina shares her favorite pasta recipe with Rona and the two exchange a few texts complimenting each other on being strong women in their relationships. Kathrina is amazed by Rona's perseverance as the single source of income to her family so that Shirley can stay home with the kids. In California, it is very difficult to have a family live comfortably on a single source of income because the cost of living is so high. Rona adores Kathrina's maternal instincts as a caregiver and is secretly attracted to her beauty. Being depraved of affection and strong support from their partners, the two continue to exchange pleasant thoughts about each other throughout the day.

Almost done with preparing Mr. Bradshaw's dinner, Kathrina notices a new message notification on her phone. Initially she's excited to see what cute or sweet thing Rona might be sending her now, but when she looks closer she realizes the message is from her sister. Calculating the time difference in her head, she is instantly mortified because it is 3:00 A.M. back home in the Philippines. Dinner is ready and Mr. Bradshaw is waiting peacefully at his table in anticipation of another Kathrina creation, but she is eager to call home and see what is on her sister's mind. She sneaks out the back door to run over and ask David to serve Mr. Bradshaw's dinner explaining to him that it's an emergency. David gives her a great deal of attitude because he has to stop playing his game but is more afraid of Mr. Bradshaw than her. He drops what he is doing and runs over to serve his dinner.

Her sister Lourdes answers on the first ring, "Hello Kathrina." Kathrina responds, "Yes Lourdes. What's going on? What happened! Why are you up?"

Getting straight to the point, Lourdes explains, "Michele is very sick. She went camping with her classmates and came back with a very high fever. We thought it was just the flu, but we couldn't get her fever under control. We brought her to the Makati Medical Center and the doctors have diagnosed her with Japanese Encephalitis. They said her brain is swelling and that she might go into a coma. I'm so scared!"

Feeling faint and weak in her knees Kathrina sits at the counter and asks, "How did she get that?" Her sister replies, "They said from mosquito bites!"

Kathrina, becoming hysterical, "Can she die from it? Do you need money!?"

Lourdes responds, "They said it's too soon to tell how her body will react. They are giving her medicine to help with pain and to treat her symptoms, but her immune system will have to fight the virus! We don't need money. I wish you were here. I need you!"

Kathrina now crying, "I'm so sorry Lourdes, you know I want to be there and that I would get on a flight tonight if I could."

Lourdes interrupts, "I know, I know . . . I'm sorry I know your status there. I'm sorry to worry you, but we need your prayers and I wanted to hear your voice. I will sleep now ok, I am so tired."

Kathrina replies, "I love you Lourdes. Please kiss Michele for me. Call me if anything changes. I don't care what time."

Lourdes reciprocates, "I love you too sister. Bye for now."

Sitting on the couch in darkness and silence, Kathrina closes her eyes and begins to pray to God to bless her niece. Right at the end of her prayer as she is saying Amen, her phone rings and its Jennifer. Jennifer greets Kathrina and can hear the distress in her voice. She inquires, "What's wrong? Are you ok?"

Kathrina responds, "My niece is very ill and if she doesn't get better she could die! She is at Makati Medical Center in Manila. I don't know what to do. To be by her side, I would have to sacrifice everything I have here."

Jennifer responds, trying to comfort her as much as possible, "Oh my goodness. I am so sorry Kathrina. I will say a prayer for her. I also know that Makati Medical Center is one of the best hospitals in Manila. I'm sure she will get the best treatment."

Kathrina thanks Jennifer for the concerns and then goes on to explain, "This is another reason why I need to fix my status here in the states. It's embarrassing always being afraid of the police and checkpoints. I hate that we can't get real jobs and that we are treated like second-class citizens. But what worries me most is that I cannot go home. I am missing my nieces and nephews growing up."

Jennifer tells Kathrina, "I've been thinking hard about your situation and spoke to Carl about it the other night. I want to propose a solution. Do you mind if I quickly bring Rona on the call?" Feeling both hesitant and anxious to know why Rona needs to be on the call Kathrina replies, "Ok."

Once both ladies are on the line, Jennifer gets straight to the point. Jennifer says, "You guys know that I love both of you. I am so happy to have Kathrina back in my life and thankful to you Rona for being such a good friend to me since I married Carl. Having you around helped me to deal with being homesick and away from my family."

Interrupting Jennifer, both Kathrina and Rona say, "I love you too," almost in unison.

Jennifer continues with her previous thought, "I listen to the challenges that each of you battle each day and I want to ask for your permission to discuss them openly between the three of us."

Waiting for verbal affirmation from Rona and Kathrina, Jennifer pauses. Kathrina replies first, "You have my permission," followed by Rona, "Sure ok."

Jennifer responds, "Thank you. So, the other night I was talking to Carl about your challenges and we think that we know a solution to both of your problems. Kathrina, you and David need legal status in the states. You need the freedom to travel and the opportunity to earn income on real jobs. Rona, you need to get out of debt so that you can focus on spending time with your family. I know this is going to sound very awkward, but what if you guys got married?"

Surprised, Kathrina responds, "WHAT!"

Jennifer replies, "Hear me out. It's not such an outrageous idea. Rona and Shirley are not married. The military has been accepting same sex marriages since 2013. Kathrina, you and Rona can get married and once you have adjusted your status to become a naturalized citizen you can file for divorce. Since Kathrina is not a lesbian and Rona is in a committed relationship with Shirley, David doesn't have to feel threatened or jealous of the arrangement. On the other hand, if you guys can come up with money to help out Rona, she can spend more time at home and less time stressing about how to make ends meet."

Concerned, Kathrina asks, "Can we get in trouble for that? It sounds like fraud."

Jennifer replies, "Love is a passion of the heart. How can an outsider judge if you guys are in love or not? What's so bad about it? People do it all the time. You are a good person. This country would benefit greatly from you becoming a citizen."

Embarrassed to be in need of financial support, Rona says, "I couldn't take money for helping a friend out. That sounds so selfish."

Jennifer replies, "You guys need to calm down. Try to think of this as a business transaction. Take the emotions out of it. Try to stay open-minded and think about the benefits and what this arrangement can do for the both of you in the long run. You don't have to make a decision tonight. Just think about it. Talk to David and Shirley and get their feedback too."

Feeling that the conversation is getting very tense, Jennifer suggest that they both sleep on the idea. Though Kathrina and Rona are both obviously concerned about all the things that could go wrong, they kindly thank Jennifer for making a proposal to end their suffering.

Kathrina lies in bed browsing WEBMD about Japanese Encephalitis, worried about all the things that could go wrong and wondering what she can do to help. Feeling helpless, she closes her eyes and begins to pray to God for mercy and deliverance. She asks for forgiveness of her sins and makes a vow to God that she will be a better person. She also meditates on the proposal that Jennifer presented and wonders if this scenario is something for which God would forgive her. She falls asleep conflicted about the principles of her Catholic faith with regard to the marriage proposal and wonders if her niece's sickness is a punishment from God. Or, is the proposal a blessing from God, which answers her prayers and allows her to freely pursue happiness in America?

Violently jumping up from a nightmare, Kathrina is breathing hard and inadvertently wakes David from a deep slumber. His immediate first impression is that Mr. Bradshaw must be demanding something. He inquires, "What is it? What does he want now?"

Kathrina replies, "Nothing, I had a really bad nightmare."

Seeing Kathrina emotionally and physically shaken, David extends his arms to embrace and comfort her. She falls into his arms, but her reaction is opposite to his expectation. She starts crying hysterically. David asks again, "What is wrong?" Kathrina tries to respond but she is crying so hard that David cannot understand a word she is saying. He is now wide awake and beginning to become mortified himself with the anticipation of finding out what could be so wrong. Softly caressing her head, he brushes his fingertips across her cheeks to wipe the tears from her face and he place his hand under her chin to raise her head and eyes to his level.

Once their eyes meet, he asks her again very calmly, "What is wrong? I am here for you. Tell me." Kathrina, only slightly calmer, replies, "Lourdes called earlier to tell me that Michelle is sick, and she might die. You know I love that girl! I always treated her as if she were my own."

David comments, "I know baby. I know. What do you mean she might die? What's wrong with her?"

Kathrina sobbing, "She has a very deadly virus that she got from a mosquito bite. Her fever is super high, and the doctors think she could go into a coma or even get brain damage from swelling."

David trying to calm Kathrina, "Baby, did you pray? I know you did. Just put your trust in God. There is nothing else we can do."

Once again David receives a reaction that he didn't expect: Kathrina yells, "There is something we could do! We could be on our way there to be by her side, but we can't! You are so content with this sorry life that we live! Where we are trapped, where we have no freedom, where we are treated like slaves!

You want this forever. I can't do this anymore, what is your plan?! How do we fix our immigration status?!"

David sits in silence with a blank expression on his face not wanting to add fuel to the fire, knowing that the best course of action for his internal peace is to remain calm and allow Kathrina to vent. Kathrina continues to dig into David, "Exactly! I knew it! You have no answers. I have to figure out everything on my own while you just have fun and treat life like some kind of video game!"

Still silent, David just stares back with puppy dog eyes. Kathrina's anger with the absence of urgency in David to fix their immigration status gives her the courage to blatantly attack David with Jennifer's proposal, "I am going to marry Rona!" David now unable to continue biting his tongue, "What!? You are going to do what!"

Now completely calm, Kathrina says, "I am going to marry Rona."

David says, "What are you talking about? She is with Shirley. What about us? You are going to leave me?!"

Kathrina replies, "No, I am going to solve our problems because you cannot. I will marry Rona so that I can become a citizen. After my status is adjusted we will divorce and I will marry you so that we can both stay here and live out our dreams."

David now feeling marginalized and threatened, "You are going to throw away our relationship to be with a lesbian just to get your papers."

Kathrina quickly responds, "That's not what I said! I am going to do this to ensure our future because you have done nothing."

David inquires, "Why would Rona do that? What is in it for her?"

With clear apathy for David, Kathrina responds, "Money."

Shortly after leaving for work and in transit to the base, Rona is excited to talk to Shirley about Jennifer's proposal but doesn't know how she will react. Stuck in traffic waiting at a train crossing for a long freight train to pass, she ponders how she should make the proposal. She shivers at the thought of telling her in person. Considering that their relationship is already a little rocky, she is worried that Shirley will become jealous of Kathrina. Then she thinks about making a phone call, but she still feels that method would be awkward and too revealing. Now contemplating the idea of drafting a text that sounds playful and "tests the waters," she picks up her phone and begins typing, "Hey baby when are we going to the beach again? I want to see your sexy body in a bikini!"

Shirley responds, "But I don't like how bikinis fit me!"

Rona types, "Baby you look good in everything that touches your body."

Shirley inquires, "Are you horny this morning? Why are you thinking about my body?"

Rona replies, "I admire your body; can we please go to the beach soon?"

Shirley responds, "We can go as soon as you find a bathing suit that conceals my flaws."

Rona now ready to take her shot, says, "Baby you are flawless, but you know I'd love to help you build your confidence. Remember when you went to get a consultation about breast augmentation? How much was the estimate for the cost of the procedure?"

Shirley becoming inquisitive, asks, "Why so many questions? It's not like we can afford it?"

Rona quickly types, "We can!"

Suddenly the cars behind Rona start honking and she realizes the train has passed and she's holding traffic. She quickly types, "I'll talk to you about it when I get home."

Excited to greet Rona after the long day at work, Shirley decides to prepare dinner for once in a blue moon. Shirley bribes the kids to go to bed early with the promise of Chuck E. Cheese after school. She carefully selects Rona's favorite Marie Calendars Pot Pie from the freezer and chills a fresh bottle of Barefoot Chardonnay. She arranges scented candles around the dining room, dims the lights, and with Sade's voice and music she sets the mood. Shirley, lying on the living room couch in her red satin negligee, anxiously awaits Rona's arrival. She grabs the cosmopolitan magazine from their table and searches for articles about the best breast augmentation doctors in Southern California.

When she hears Rona's keys turning the locks she jumps up to greet her at the door, "Hello Boo. I missed you so much." She leans in for a juicy kiss on Rona's full lips. Rona reacts by caressing the back Shirley's head pressing gently to apply more pressure to their lips. From her other hand, she drops the keys and her backpack, and the two lovers stumble over to the couch not separating their lips for a moment. On the couch, Rona becomes more aggressive and begins fondling Shirley's breast. Shirley now becoming self-conscious of her tiny breast pulls away from Rona and says, "Baby, I made you dinner."

Rona still coming on to her in an aggressive manner, says seductively, "I don't care about dinner. I want you!"

Shirley replies, "You know I never cook. I know you are hungry and tired, let me serve you. We can play afterwards."

Rona, slightly disappointed, agrees to change into something more comfortable so that she can join Shirley for a pseudo-romantic dinner. Rona enjoys her pot pie and sipping wine starts to tear down her inhibitions, she asks Shirley, "Why do you get so self-conscious when I touch your breast."

Shirley replies, "Because I've always been embarrassed about having small boobs and I wish my breast were at least a hand full."

Rona replies, "You know I think your body is beautiful. I have a proposal that I think could help us. Will you listen with an open mind?"

Shirley responds, "Of course, I love you."

Rona continues, "Jennifer and Carl suggested that we help Kathrina and David become citizens. They will in return pay us for helping them."

Confused, Shirley asks, "How are we going to help them?"

Contrary to Rona's usual bravado and aggressiveness, she responds in a very demure manner, "I'll marry Kathrina."

Shirley responds, "How much are they going to pay us? How are they going to pay in check or cash?"

Rona replies, "We haven't negotiated an agreement on payment yet. I'll have another call with Kathrina and Jennifer and we will start negotiating, but I wanted to know how you felt about it."

Shirley responds, "I am ok with that. A boob job, shopping money, and that soul-searching journey that I have always wanted to the Caribbean is worth it!"

Shirley, once again excited, grabs Rona's hand and leads her to the bedroom where they continue from where they left off in the living room before dinner.

In the morning, David is on the couch cheering for the LA Rams and Kathrina is bored sitting next to him chatting with her siblings on Viber chat. She is happy to hear that Michelle's health has improved and her condition has been downgraded from intensive care to critical care. The doctors are now very optimistic because her fever has broken, and she seems to be getting stronger hour after hour. Kathrina is extremely happy and says a little prayer to thank God. Uncharacteristically, she cheers for the Rams right along with David as they score touchdowns.

Rona and Shirley have slept in and are in bed cuddling tightly. The kids are running around the house, making noises and playing games. They are being kids, fighting over toys, laughing loudly, and bumping around the house like a jackhammer at a construction project. Rona and Shirley are able to block out the noises until one of the kids starts banging on the door to collect on the bribe Shirley made the night prior. Little James incessantly rapping on the door yells, "Mommy, when are we going to Chuck E. Cheese's? You promised!" Rona wakes up and looking through blurred sleepy eyes asks Shirley, "You promised them Chuck E. Cheese? We will never rest now!"

Shirley giggling, "A girls has to do, what a girl has to do It worked right? Last night was definitely worth it to me." Rona affirms her sentiments with a smile and soft kiss on Shirley forehead.

Carl and Jennifer are up early and jogging together at the park. Jennifer breaks the news to Carl that she made the proposal to Rona and Kathrina the night before. He almost trips mid-stride and comes to a stop to ask Jennifer, "Oh my goodness, you did? How did it go?"

Jennifer stops and still out of breath tries to explain, "Well, at first they were both skeptical of the idea." She leans over and places her hands on her knees and Carl offers her water from his runner's fanny pack saying, "Sorry honey, catch your breath. Here's some water. You want to sit down? Come over to this bench so we can talk."

With the biggest grin on his face he leads her to sit down. Jennifer opens up and says, "They were supposed to talk to their significant others and get back to me today. Towards the end of the conversation it seemed that they were both open to the idea."

Carl replies, "Why didn't you tell me? You should have called them this morning instead of coming on this jog. I'm so anxious to see how this unfolds. Let's finish up this run so you can call them."

Back at home and fresh out of the shower, Jennifer makes the call to Rona.

Rona answers, "Hi Jennifer."

Jennifer inquires, "Hi Rona, did you and Shirley have time to talk it out?"

Hearing the sound of games and the voices of strange kids in the background, Jennifer asks, "Can you talk? Where are you?"

Rona replies, "Oh we are at Chuck E. Cheese's. It's ok, we can talk if you can hear me. The kids are just playing."

Jennifer says, "Well? What do you think?"

Rona without hesitation says, "We want to do it. We had a very productive discussion last night," giggling while looking at Shirley.

Laughing Jennifer responds, "I take it that you guys had a little celebration about the proposal."

Rona says, "Something like that."

Jennifer, wanting to get to business, asks, "So did you guys think about a number? How much do you think that you will charge them for the arrangement?"

Rona says, "Hold on." She mutes her phone and asks Shirley what she thinks. Shirley has obviously been thinking about the topic and has no shame in responding, "$30,000 dollars."

Rona's eyes open wide and she gasps, "Really!? You think they can afford that?"

Shirley says, "That's not our concern! You know my plans for that money. Don't be shy! Closed mouths don't get fed."

Now with hesitation and a little shame, Rona unmutes the phone and answer's Jennifer's question hoping it's not a deal breaker, "We want $30,000 dollars."

Jennifer sitting on her couch puts her hand on her forehead in disbelief knowing that Shirley is manipulating her friend and replies, "Ok, I'll call Kathrina now and see if they can come up with that much money. Can you hold on for a moment?"

With the Ram's game at halftime, Kathrina and David are in good spirits and talking about the proposal again. David is feeling like Kathrina is internally apologetic about her attitude the previous night and he is feeling closer to her now than they have been in a while. He leans in to give her a kiss when Kathrina's phone begins ringing.

She answers, "Hello?"

Jennifer and Rona respond in unison, "Hi."

Kathrina, hearing two voices, looks down at her caller id for validation and inquires, "Jennifer? Is that you?"

Jennifer responds, "It's me and Rona. You know why we are calling, right?"

Kathrina replies, "Yes, but hold on."

Kathrina mutes the phone and leans in to finish what David started. She gives him a sensual and soft kiss and assures him, "Baby I love you. This is Rona and Jennifer. We have to give them an answer. Are you ok with this?"

Feeling the pressure and wanting to fulfill Kathrina's greatest wish he replies, "Yes. I'll do it for you."

Now ecstatic, Kathrina unmutes the phone and says, "We will do it! What is the next step? When can we start?"

Jennifer interjects with, "The first step is an agreement on the amount you will pay Rona. She has a number."

Still excited and expecting mercy, Kathrina is quick to say, "Ok, whatever it takes! Tell me how much you want Rona."

Rona replies, "We need $30,000 dollars."

Taking a deep breath and with a knot in her throat, she replies without taking a timeout to huddle with David, "We can get $30,000."

David's eyes open wide and to avoid losing his temper or yelling he decides to walk away and get a beer.

Jennifer then replies, "Ok now that we have that settled, I guess the next question will be how you will distribute the funds. To keep things as fair and transparent as possible, Carl suggested that the payments be distribute in four phases: a small deposit now to get started; a progress payment when the wedding license is filed; a progress payment when the INS documents are filed; and the final payment once Kathrina's status has been adjusted. Does that sound fair?"

Rona replies, "Yes."

Kathrina follows with, "That works for me."

Jennifer inquires, "How soon do you guys want to get started? How much time do you need to get the money?"

Quick to respond Kathrina replies, "We have $5,000 in savings right now. I don't want to delay the process a single day. Can we meet tonight at Jennifer's house?"

Rona and Shirley have no squabbles with making time to meet at Jennifer's. Jennifer is very anxious to get this started agrees without getting Carl's clearance, knowing that he would approve.

After the call, Kathrina notices that David hasn't returned to finish watching the game. Instead, he is in his man cave playing video games. She walks over to him and explains that they will need to raise $30,000. David is giving her little attention out of anger at her relentless pursuit to adjust their immigration status without his buy-in or approval. Kathrina being persistent to get his attention tells him that she is going to Venmo the money and head over to Jennifer's house to iron out the details. David still acts oblivious to her and continues to play his game.

He looks up from the game and says one thing, "Do what you have to do, you don't have to involve me."

She responds, "You know I have to involve you. We only have $5,000 in the bank now."

David, transferring his focus back to the game, dryly replies, "You know I can get it from my parents. I just have to ask. Seems like you have made up your mind. I'll call them later."

David has checked out and is in his fantasy game world. Not wanting to nag David to take her to Jennifer's house, she lets him know that she will drive herself there. After she gets dressed, she sends a text to Rona inviting her to connect via Venmo. Rona accepts immediately and Kathrina executes the money transfer. Rona responds, "Nice doing business with you, I'll see you at Jennifer's house later."

The three ladies are sitting outside on Carl and Jennifer's patio sipping wine around the fire pit. Jennifer explains, "I'm so excited about this wedding.

I've already begun planning it for you. I've done my homework and I think the easiest and most affordable option is for us to do it in Vegas."

Kathrina raises her glass and jokingly states, "Cheers to eloping to Vegas! My dream wedding."

Rona and Jennifer raise their glasses. Kathrina continues, "What did you have planned?"

Jennifer explains, "Its simple. I'll book a room at the Palazzo and we will have your bachelorette party there. We will have dinner, go dancing and have a few drinks to loosen up. We have to apply for a marriage license at the Clark County Marriage Bureau by midnight and then the wedding chapel is open 24 hours. There is no waiting period. We can literally get the license in fifteen minutes and stand in line to see the minister right after. The whole process will take less than an hour during off-peak times."

Rona replies, "Funny that it's so easy to get married, but so hard to get divorced. So, when are we doing this? Next weekend?"

Jokingly, Kathrina says, "I just filled my gas tank, we can go now." They all look at each other and start laughing uncontrollably.

Carl walks out to see what's the ruckus. He inquires, "What is so funny? Please share."

Jennifer tells Carl, "Kathrina suggested that we drive to Vegas and tie the knot now."

He responds, "Hmmm, you know what. I think I have some comps that are for weekdays only. If you drive out there tonight, you can check in at the Pallazzo on Monday for free."

Now truly intrigued, the ladies are hanging on to every single word Carl says. He continues, "Kathrina might be on to something. Why not take advantage? Plus, you won't have to stand in line at the marriage bureau or at the wedding chapel."

As quickly as Carl walked into the conversation he walks out as if he just dropped the mic on stage in a rap battle. The ladies are left to ponder his suggestion. The bride-to-be is anxious to get this done so she volunteers to drive the entire trip if they are up to it. Rona and Jennifer look at each other and Rona says, "What the hell! You only live once. Let's go. I will call my commanding officer and let him know that I have a family emergency. I never have trouble getting time off because I am always at work."

Jennifer says, "My husband just gave me a Vegas pass, I'm not passing up on that. I'm down for a little crazy."

The ladies all run and pack away their necessities for a quick turnaround trip. Excitement and adrenaline fuel Kathrina as she makes the long-haul drive to Vegas. The rising sun causes her to squint as the 15 Freeway descends into the Las Vegas valley. Only now is she beginning to feel the effects of the long ride. She wakes up Rona and Jennifer to keep her company and awake for the final leg of the trip. They check into the hotel and carry their things up to the room where Kathrina passes out immediately from the exhaustion of driving throughout the night. Rona and Jennifer decide to go have a bite to eat and then spend some time lying out by the pool.

Kathrina sleeps most of the day and wakes up just as the sun is beginning to set. Rona and Jennifer are in disbelief by the amount of time it takes Kathrina to recharge but are happy that she is awake so that the festivities can begin. Jennifer and Kathrina spend hours perfecting their makeup and outfits in the restroom while Rona is happy sporting her newest La Coste polo shirt and cargo pants. She decides to go down into the casino to try her luck at slots and have a couple of drinks while she waits for them to get ready. Rona is raking in a nice purse at the slots when she is ambushed by Jennifer and Kathrina. She is immediately amazed by how beautiful and sexy Kathrina looks. She is speechless, but her wide eyes and chin drop tell the whole story.

Jennifer jokes, "Ok love birds, are you ready for this? Our dinner reservations are at seven. I was thinking we would go to the marriage bureau at eleven. That gives us an hour to complete the paperwork and then head over to the chapel."

Rona states, "Sounds like a plan," and grabs her bride by the hand.

Looking at Jennifer she says, "Shouldn't you be taking pictures or something? You are our witness!"

Rona and Kathrina pose for their first picture together as a couple standing in front of the Vegas Eiffel Tower on their way to dinner. Rona whispers in Kathrina's ear as Jennifer is snapping the shot, "The idea of traveling through the streets of Paris with a beautiful woman is as romantic as it gets."

Rona then plants an innocent kiss on Kathrina blushing cheek. Jennifer is in full on paparazzi mode capturing the moments for evidence. They have an exquisite dinner, followed by dancing and a few drinks. As the night expires and it is getting closer to the moment of truth, Kathrina is visibly disturbed and slightly withdrawn. In the cab ride over to the marriage bureau she is on her phone texting the entire time. Rona and Jennifer give her space as they hold a conversation about Shirley's plans for the money.

They arrive at the marriage bureau and on the stairway up into the building, Kathrina stops in her tracks.

Both Rona and Jennifer look back and Jennifer asks, "What's wrong did you forget something in the cab?"

Kathrina replies, "No, it's not that!" Rona walks over and grabs her hand. In her sweetest semi-macho voice, she says, "It's ok. I'm not going to bite you," and starts laughing out loud.

However, Kathrina doesn't seem entertained. In fact, she begins crying and turns to walk away saying, "I can't do this."

Rona and Jennifer are left standing there in total shock. Jennifer looks to Rona and says, "I wonder what happened." They both run to catch up with her with open arms to comfort.

Rona responds, "It's ok. It's ok. Don't be sad. If it isn't meant to be, it isn't meant to be. Calm down."

Kathrina fighting back tears says, "I can't do this without David's support. I've been trying to call and text him all day. I've barely gotten a response. I'm afraid to be without him and I'm afraid of us being caught up in an investigation for fraud."

However, secretly in Kathrina's heart she knows those are only cursory concerns. What she fears most of all is her growing attraction to Rona. Rona has been more of a man to her on this trip than David has been for the past several years. She actually enjoyed the romantic whisperings and soft kisses. Unlike her time with David, with Rona she feels she is the star of the show and the center of attention. Rona makes her feel like a princess. She looks to her like a knight in shining armor, her hero and place of comfort. Confused by her feelings, Kathrina cries until she falls asleep in the cab.

Rona, needing to get back to work and not wanting to waste any more time in Vegas, convinces Jennifer and Kathrina that they should check out early and get back on the road. Rona decides to drive because Kathrina is still emotionally depressed. She sleeps virtually the entire way home. Jennifer gently nudges Kathrina when they arrive at Mr. Bradshaw's house and says, "Sweetheart we are home. Here are your keys; Rona is going to drive us back to the base now. Do you want us to walk you to the door?"

Kathrina not wanting to impose any more, declines the offer and tells them to drive home safely.

David is in bed fast asleep when Kathrina walks in wearing her wedding gown. He is awakened by the sound of her arrival. Still half asleep, he turns on the bed side lamp and says, "Wow aren't you a pretty bride!?"

His eyes still adjusting as she comes into focus he realizes that her eyes are puffy and her mascara is ruined.

He inquires, "What's wrong baby? Why aren't you happy?"

She replies, "David I need you. I'm so sorry I forced you to do this."

He responds, "What are you talking about?"

Kathrina replies, "I didn't do it."

David, not able to contain himself, slowly starts to boil: "What do you mean you didn't do it? You already transferred our money to them. You have to do it!"

Kathrina inquires, "Why didn't you respond to my calls and messages while I was gone?" David simply says, "I was busy. That's it. Just playing games and watching TV. I went to bed early. I can't believe you didn't do it! I know how much you want this and it took us a long time to save that much money. Call Rona now. I want to talk to her!"

Kathrina, never seeing David so angry and aggressive, becomes fearful of what he might say to her, but she passes him the phone anyway. Rona answers on speakerphone with Jennifer in the car, "Hey Kathrina, are you ok?"

David responds, "She's fine. This is David."

Rona surprised replies, "Oh, hey David."

Straight to the point, David says, "Since Kathrina couldn't do it, I propose that you and I get married. Is the deal still on the table?"

Chapter 8: Holy Matrimony

The thought of losing Kathrina's affection has created an unprecedented sense of urgency in David. Almost overnight he has matured into a responsible, ambitious, and determined man. Determined to do whatever it will take to win the love and affection of Kathrina. Determined to find a way to give her the life that she dreams of.

Kathrina awakens to find herself in bed alone. She can faintly hear David's voice in the distance as she walks down the hall to start her morning routine, but this morning is particularly different. There are no explosions, no swearing, no gunshots, no loud childish celebrations. Instead she finds David at his desk working on the computer and engaged in what appears to be a serious conversation. Kathrina is in such shock by his unusual behavior that she can't think clearly. She bumbles around the kitchen, a scatter brain. Looking in the pantry for milk to put in her coffee, opening the freezer to grab a coffee mug. The curiosity to figure out what is going on has her completely distracted. She listens intently to reconnoiter his actions. She wonders, has he decided he's not going to take her shit anymore? Is he leaving her? Is there some kind of family emergency? Has someone died?

David speaking to his mom, "Hey Ma. I'm engaged!"

"Hay Naku, David. What are you talking about?" replies his mother.

David reasserts, "Ma I'm getting married!"

His mother replies in disbelief, "David are you serious?"

David in his serious voice states, "Yes Ma. I'm getting married."

David's mom begins to cry and yell out to everyone in the house, "My baby is getting married. Finally…he's getting married."

In the background David can hear his dad and grandma getting excited. He is the last of his siblings to make a serious move toward adulthood.

David's dad asking to speak to his son, "Son I'm so proud of you!"

David replies, "Thank you, dad."

Snatching the phone back from her husband, David's mom continues, "It's about time! Don't tell me you are getting married because Kathrina is pregnant!"

Before David can respond, "Let me talk to my daughter-in-law to be! I want to congratulate her."

David replies, "Mom and dad please calm down. I'm getting married, but it's not to Kathrina."

In shock his mom says, "What are you talking about? Then WHOM?"

David replies, "It's a business transaction. We are going to fix our immigration status. Once we fix it, then we will marry each other."

Disappointed but still intrigued, "So you are getting married to someone else who is a citizen there?"

David responds, "Yes Ma."

David's dad pulls the phone away from his mom, "Whom are you marrying? Can we trust this person to not take advantage of us?"

In response to his dad's concern, "Yes dad, it is a safe arrangement. She is mutual friend of Kathrina and one of her high school friends. She is also in the Air Force. I trust her to keep her word. You don't have to worry."

Still concerned, dad inquires, "Who's idea is this? Will Kathrina become jealous? You will be married to another woman and will have to keep up the appearance that you are married."

David dismisses his concerns by explaining, "Dad this lady is in a committed relationship with another woman. She is a lesbian. So, there will be nothing to be jealous about and no temptations."

David's parents have mixed feelings about this arrangement but understand that this might be the only possible way for their son and Kathrina to remain in the States legally. Becoming more inquisitive about the details, David's dad continues, "I know this is going to cost you something. Before I settled down with your mom I was going to marry one of your uncle's friends so that I could go to the states. She wanted $10,000 and that was in the '70s. How much are you paying this lesbian?"

David replies, "Well dad that's one of the reasons for my call. We cannot do this on our own. I need your support both financially and as witnesses. The lesbian couple is asking us to pay $30,000. I already made a deposit of $5,000."

David's dad replies, "You know we are here to support you. Just let us know how and when we can help." David thanks his parents and explains to them that he will be in touch soon with more details.

David spins around in his chair and is startled to find that Kathrina has been sitting quietly on the couch behind him. She jumps up and with excitement grabs him tightly to embrace him and thank him for taking the lead and completing what she started. Holding him tightly, she whispers in his ear. "Thank you baby. I love you so much. I couldn't do it because I was worried about our future. I didn't feel I had your support."

David replies, "Ganda, I know how much this means to you. I'm sorry that I have been taking you for granted for so long. I want to do what makes you happy and what is best for our future." Kathrina kisses David with renewed passion.

Afterwards, David inquires jokingly, "So what was the plan? What were the steps that you guys discussed? Do I get a honeymoon? Will I carry Rona across the threshold? I'm probably going to need to start working out, huh?"

Kathrina giggles and gives him another peck on the lips before she gives him the rundown on how the Vegas wedding works. David replies, "Sounds simple enough!"

Later that afternoon, David is out with Mr. Bradshaw for his annual check-up. Kathrina decides to check in with the girls. She calls Jennifer first, but she is busy with the kids and the call goes to voicemail.

On the voicemail Kathrina says, "Hi Jennifer, this is Kathrina I'm calling to apologize to you for being a runaway bride. I know how much thought that both you and Carl put into helping us. Please call me when you get a moment. Thank you."

In leaving the message to Kathrina, she is reminded by how embarrassing and cowardly her actions were in Vegas. She is ashamed to call Rona on the phone. Instead she prepares and sends a text, "Hi. Rona I am so sorry about my cowardice in Vegas. I am so ashamed to face you after wasting your time."

She hits send and before she can gather her thoughts for the next message, she sees that Rona is drafting a reply. Kathrina waits in suspense for what feels like an eternity.

Rona replies, "We were really looking forward to that money. David said he will take your place. Are we still moving forward? I need to give Shirley and answer."

Kathrina can't help but feel that the small flame that had been kindled between them was completely snuffed out. This deal is now purely transactional. Rona is under extreme pressure to solve her financial woes and to satisfy her trophy girlfriend. She is no longer concerned with any secret desires for romantic escapes with Kathrina.

Kathrina responds to Rona's text, "Yes, we are moving forward. David is arranging for his parents to come be our witnesses. Can we do this in like two weeks?"

Before Rona can respond, Kathrina receives an incoming call from Jennifer.

Katrina answers, "Hi Jennifer, did you get my message?"

Jennifer sounding a little annoyed and lacking patience, "Yes, I got it. I'm busy with the kids working on a science project. What's up?"

Kathrina sensing Jennifer's disappointment is very brief, "I've been texting Rona. Even though I backed out, we are going to move forward, and David will marry her. What do you think about that?"

Jennifer being extremely short responds, "Good luck!"

Feeling the conversation is very awkward and that she has strained the relationship, Kathrina apologizes again and invites Jennifer and Carl to come to Vegas for the second wedding as their special guest.

Jennifer sounding extremely unimpressed explains, "Sorry Kathrina, Carl and I will be visiting his parents. We cannot attend the wedding. Hey, I've got to catch up with you later. The kids are making a mess!"

Before Kathrina can say another word, the call is disconnected, and she reads the last message sent by Rona: "Yes. Can we do it the weekend after next? I don't have many more paid days off."

Kathrina replies, "Sure. We can do whatever is convenient to you. I will talk to David and his parents about final details and I will let you know. Thanks for giving us another chance."

Rona responds, "Thank you. We are helping each other. TTYL I have to get back to work."

David walks in from a long day with Mr. Bradshaw at the doctor's office and is greeted at the door by the smell of his favorite meal. Kathrina has prepared one of her specialties, the ultimate comfort dish, Sinigang. Subconsciously, David is immediately transported to his grandma's house at Easter time: a house full of family, friends, love and fun. The huge smile on David's face gives Kathrina instant gratification for her hard work. He kisses Kathrina on the forehead and rushes off to freshen up for dinner. At dinner David and Kathrina further discuss the plans for the marriage. ogether they choose the day and decide to follow the same plan that Jennifer had outlined with one change, this wedding will be held during the day with a more traditional backdrop than a sin city type of elopement. They will rent a tux for the David and a gown for Rona, David's mom will escort him down the aisle and his dad will escort Rona, Kathrina will be Rona's maid of honor, and one of David's buddies from basketball will be the best man. David and Kathrina will purchase inexpensive wedding bands and she will arrange coordinating flowers to decorate a boutonniere for David's coat and a bouquet for Rona to carry. They have completed their meals, but the conversation at the dinner table continues. David grabs his iPad and together they book a professional photographer, start shopping rates at the hotels, and choose a restaurant where they will host their mini reception. David calls his parents to make sure that his benefactors are ready and willing to make their plan a reality.

Arriving at McCarran International and back in the states after many years, David's parents are excited about visiting Las Vegas for the first time. Fresh off the jetway at the airline gate, David's dad is overcome with the temptation to try his luck at a slot machine. He hurries over to the money exchange to trade his pesos for dollars and grabs mom's hand to drag her in tow to the slot machine. She passively objects by pulling in the opposite direction and walking slowly, but David's dad is on a mission. On his first few spins he is just whetting his appetite for the excitement of gambling and learning the payouts. On his third try he exclaims, "Third try is a charm!" No jackpot. On his seventh try he exclaims, "Seven is my lucky number." No jackpot.

By his thirteenth try, mom exclaims, "If we don't go now we are not only going to lose dollars, we are going to lose our luggage. Let's go!"

He agrees and the couple makes their way to the baggage claim carousel where they are greeted by the most unanticipated of welcome parties: a group of missionaries offering Bibles, Prayers and Christian Fellowship to remind them that God loves them. The leader of the group asks David's mom, "How long are your visiting?"

She replies, "We are leaving next week."

The missionary hands her a business card and invites them to worship with them on Sunday. David's mom smiles, thanks the missionaries, and as they are walking away looks to David's dad with the most puzzled look.

With a grin on her face, "I didn't expect that we would be greeted this way! We did land in Las Vegas, right?" David shows up at the baggage claim area just as they are collecting their bags. He hugs his mom like a kid that had been dropped off on the first day of kindergarten and tells her that he misses her. David hugs his dad and grabs his bags to help carry them out to the parking lot. Looking over David's should, his dad sees Kathrina and Rona walking over to them in the terminal. He whispers to David, "Son that's Kathrina, is the other one your fiancé?"

David replies, "Yes dad."

David introduces Rona to his parents and on the car ride to the hotel they discuss the financial terms of their agreement and the expectations for the next couple of days in Vegas. Once they reach the Vegas strip all focus is out the window as David and Kathrina's plans are just background noise to David's parents who are in awe of the beauty and grandeur of the structures and monuments; the vast supply and diversity of shopping options; the density of tourists in the streets; and all the billboards promoting popular shows, fabulous meals, and suggestive adult themed fun. Driving, David is unable to see that he has lost his parent's attention to the strip. He searches for verbal acknowledge by inquiring, "Dad you got it? Will you and mom be ready?"

David's dad responds, "Huh, for what? Dinner?" David laughs and replies, "Dad, I was talking about the wedding plans? Everything is planned for tomorrow morning."

Despite having spent virtually the entire night gambling and drinking on the casino floor, David's parents are up at sunrise like two farmers preparing to take care of their chores so that they can enjoy the rest of the day. The wedding party assembles in the hotel lobby and David summons their limo driver to take them to the chapel. On the ride over to the chapel everyone is at ease and engaged in light conversation about which buffet they will visit afterwards.

Rona sarcastically jokes to the group while her eyes are resting on Kathrina, "David you aren't going to leave me at the altar, are you?"

Everyone starts laughing and David replies, "No dear, in fact we should be taking photos!"

In the limo SUV everyone shifts seats so that Rona and David can be seated next to each other. Kathrina grabs her cellphone and take a few quick shots of the two toasting wine glasses from the limo mini bar. They arrive at the chapel and on the stairs Kathrina has a brief dramatic moment where she flashes back to the moment she bailed out on Rona. The emotions hit her hard and tears start to well up in her eyes because for that moment she is reminded of the small flame that was building between her and Rona. She represses those feelings deep inside and continues to make her way up the stairs, hopeful that they will never return.

David notices the tears in her eyes and whispers in her ear, "Baby you know this is all for show! Don't cry. This is what you want. Soon this will be over. Remember, I love you."

They meet the photographer in the foyer of the chapel and commence to documenting the union of David and Rona. They take picture after picture of staged scenes with the wedding party. Every cast member in character and playing their role as if they are professional thespians. From the surface, everyone appears sincere. David's parents appear proud of their son; the maid of honor and best man are excited and standing by the side of the bride and groom. The bride and groom appear to be fully engaged and excited about the moment. The motivation of money, freedom, and love for someone other than each other is fueling the manifested commitment and sudden but false infatuation between the bride and groom.

Now in the moment of truth, standing before the chaplain, Kathrina's knees are shaking and she is once again stricken with emotion and a lot of anxiety. The reading of the wedding sermon feels like it is going by in slow motion. The chaplain's voice similar to the low murmuring sound of the adults' voices in the peanuts cartoons. The words are not discernible. She hears, "Wa Wa Wa Wa" until David says, "I do." Kathrina wakes from what feels like a dream, to the reality of David kissing Rona and the chaplain announcing them husband and wife.

Chapter 9: Betrayal

Back home and sitting on the couch together, David and Kathrina are watching TV. During a commercial break Kathrina jokingly asks David, "How does it feel to be married?"

David responds, "Feels like we will be getting our papers soon."

Kathrina replies, "Yes baby it does. Soon we can live the life we deserve together. You know we still have a lot of work to do. We have to convince the Department of Homeland security that this is a consummate marriage."

An oblivious David sitting like a deer caught in headlights responds, "Consummate marriage? You mean I have to have sex with Rona? You're ok with that?"

Kathrina speaking through a big grin, "You really think Rona would sleep with you? She really thinks guys are gross."

David inquires, "Then what do you mean by consummating the marriage?"

Kathrina explains, "Before the DHS issues you a green card they will conduct an investigation to ensure that this marriage is real. We will need to show evidence and you guys have to get to know each other very well to pass an interview."

As the commercial break ends David loses interest in the conversation and his focus is back on his favorite television show.

Having not spoken to Jennifer since the wedding, Kathrina decides to call and say hi. It is unusual to her that Jennifer has not sent her a text or called in over a week. Their reunion had been on a such a fast track to BFF status. Since moving away from her family, she has found that it is really difficult to find good friends who sincerely care about you. Kathrina is hopeful that she can regain Jennifer's favor and continue the friendship with the challenges of the wedding now behind them.

Jennifer answers the call in a dry tone, "Hi Kathrina."

Kathrina responds, "Hello friend, I miss you."

Surprising Kathrina, Jennifer responds, "I miss you too."

Kathrina seizes the opportunity to offer her most sincere apology, "Jennifer you know I appreciate everything that you did for me. I'm so sorry that things didn't work out the way that you'd originally planned for me."

Jennifer interrupts, "It's ok. I'm sorry for getting upset with you. I can only imagine what was going through your mind at that moment. I was probably too pushy. I wasn't thinking about your emotions. I'm just happy for you that everything worked out ok in the end."

Jennifer goes on to ask about the ceremony and for the details that she missed. Kathrina jokingly explains that David's wedding was far more extravagant and romantic than hers could have ever been.

Jennifer responds, "Well it's easy to improve things after a trial run. The failed wedding wasn't a total waste of time after all."

Kathrina acknowledges this to be a true fact and expresses her gratitude to Jennifer once again for coming up with the original idea. Jennifer, not wanting to be a downer but wanting to make sure that Kathrina is aware that there is still a long road ahead before they get their papers, explains that the marriage is the easy part. The challenge will be convincing a DHS investigator that the marriage is legitimate.

Jennifer asks, "When are you guys going to start planning activities and staging your lives to make it appear that David and Rona are truly married? You guys will need witnesses to also contribute to your story. Carl and I were planning an outing to the Getty Museum with the kids. Would you guys like to come?"

Without hesitation Kathrina responds, "Yes, I have always wanted to go there. David is not into art or history at all. This will be my chance to convince him to come because it will help our immigration case. I'll contact Rona and make sure she can make it."

On the tram up to the Getty Center, Kathrina is transformed into a virtual paparazzi snapping pictures of Rona and David. As they disembark just outside of the museum, Kathrina is already posting the pictures to the fictitious Facebook and Instagram accounts that they created to record the "holy matrimony." Jennifer and Carl the only two followers, as of yet, to these feeds receive the notification and Carl is annoyed that they are lagging and late to arrive. Jennifer and Carl have been waiting at the entrance to the museum for nearly an hour. The kids have become anxious and are climbing on everything in sight. Carl's patience is wearing thin as he paces complaining to Jennifer, "I knew inviting them was a bad idea. This was supposed to be our family fun time and here we tangled in their web of lies, held hostage by our desires to help them out."

Jennifer apologizes to Carl, "I'm sorry baby. At least we know they are here now."

Needing to satisfy the kids' urges to run wild, the group stops at the Getty Center Gardens first. Carl runs off into the hedge maze challenging the kids to come find him. The beautiful gardens are the perfect backdrop for staged photos. Kathrina and Jennifer spring into action directing the actions of Rona and David, "Stand here, smile, kiss, hug, ok look into each other eyes, now hold hands, look over your shoulder."

Their orders rival those of the top cover girl photographers. David constantly checking his watch during the photoshoot is not impressed with the Getty Center. Growing impatient with taking photos, he urges everyone, "Can we move on? Isn't there more to see."

Suddenly, Carl and the kids emerge from the maze garden laughing and visibly fatigued from running around. Carl suggests to the group, "Let's go inside one of the pavilions. We need the A/C to cool down. Kids, it's time to learn some history!"

Now inside the first pavilion the kids are intrigued by the sculptures and antiquities. Carl and Jennifer follow closely to ensure that they behave and to help curate what they are seeing. David, Rona and Kathrina drag alone behind with Kathrina capturing random shots of David and Rona standing at the different exhibits. Oddly, David has lost interest before the kids and is texting his buddies on the basketball team to see what time their game starts. Realizing that its possible for him to make it to their game in time, he looks to Kathrina and begs to be excused, "Kathrina, do you think that we have enough pictures? If I leave now, I can get back in time for my basketball game. Can Rona bring you home?"

Before Kathrina can dispute David's proposal, Rona replies, "I'll gladly bring her home."

David anxiously waiting for Kathrina's approval, stands with his hands in a praying fashion. Kathrina replies in a sarcastically annoyed tone, "Go ahead. I'll just keep your wife company."

Walking from one pavilion to the next, Carl and Jennifer are working hard to keep the kids engaged. Looking back they see that Rona and Kathrina are lagging behind. Carl yells out, "Hey you guys, you take your time. We are going to finish up in the pavilions, call Jennifer if you need anything. Otherwise, See you next time."

Kathrina now getting the hint that she and Rona are presenting a challenge to the kids' fun, replies, "Ok. Go ahead. We are going to grab some food and sit in the garden."

Carl and Jennifer head over to the family room with the kids where they work as a team to create their own piece of art to take home and place over the fireplace. Meanwhile, Kathrina and Rona are sipping glasses of wine and eating cheese and grapes near the rose garden. Kathrina jokes, "I feel like a Roman Empress! The architecture, the food, the wine, the views, and the culture! This place is awesome."

Rona laughs and replies, "If you are the Roman empress, what does that make me? Am I your loyal slave or handmaiden? Am I to tend to your beck and call?"

Before Kathrina can respond, Rona picks a small wild flower from the grass and places it gently over Kathrina's ear. She states, "Pretty flower for a pretty lady."

Kathrina blushes, "Well thank you."

The two ladies toast to the peaceful serenity of the garden when Kathrina receives a text from Jennifer stating that she and the family are heading home.

Kathrina and Rona have been trapped in a vacuum of flirtation and the passing of time has escaped them as a golden sun is setting on the horizon.

Swerving to avoid hitting the car in front of her, a distracted Rona is feverishly texting Shirley. Kathrina concerned for their safety interjects, "Rona can that wait? If it's an emergency, why don't you pull over?"

Rona replies, "I'm sorry."

Rona puts her phone down and places her eyes on the road. There's silence in the car as Kathrina has fallen asleep and left Rona to face the snail-paced Los Angeles traffic on her own. Inching along three feet at a time along the 405, she is itching to read the message replies from Shirley. Upon hearing Kathrina's light sleep transform into a deep slumber accompanied by snoring, Rona gives into the temptation to check her messages. She lifts her phone to find cold message from Shirley, "You are easily replaceable. Fulfill the promises you made, or I'll move on to my next opportunity. I'm tired of your excuses. Where is the money? When can I book my appointment for the augmentation?"

Rona's eyes fill with tears as she is coming to the realization that Shirley's shallow desires have trumped the supposed love that binds them. Quietly weeping she responds, "I'll make a partial car payment this month and give you the rest of the money from Kathrina's deposit. That should be enough to get you started with the doctor. Ok?"

Shirley replies with a happy face emoji. The happy face emoji gives her only slight relief from an overriding feeling of irrelevance. Distracted once again, she looks up to see that the truck in front of her has suddenly stopped and she slams on her brakes. Kathrina wakes and is initially startled by the near miss accident but is immediately aware of the fact that Rona is in palpable emotional distress. She pleads with Rona to pull over. As soon as the car is safely parked, Kathrina embraces her tightly to comfort her from the source of distress. Offering her shoulder as a place of refuge for Rona's weary head and mind, Kathrina strokes her head and assures Rona that everything will be ok.

Rona hysterically states, "Shirley only cares about money. She doesn't appreciate anything I do for her. The sacrifices I make to give her and the kids a comfortable home, the fact that I turn a blind eye to her flirting with men, or the efforts to make our family financially solvent! She only cares about her shopping sprees and the money for her boob job!"

Kathrina replies, "Its ok Rona, Shirley would be crazy to risk losing you. What does she have without you? Who is going to help her take care of her kids?"

Rona responds, "She can manipulate any man or woman for that matter! She has me wrapped around her finger."

For a second time, Kathrina assures Rona that everything is going to work out. She reiterates the amount of money that she and David are giving her and tries to rationalize Shirley's behavior in the most optimistic of lights. She then extends an invitation to Rona to join her and David for dinner once they get home.

Helping clean the table, Rona is thankful to Kathrina and David for hosting her at dinner. She compliments Kathrina, "There isn't a Pinoy restaurant in town that I would choose over your cooking." She looks to David and says, "I don't know how you aren't obese. You must have a fast metabolism."

David starts giggling and replies, "Yes, I do. Otherwise, you're right. I would probably be a fat slob."

A modest and bashful Kathrina attempts to shift the focus from her cooking and makes a novel suggestion, "How about we play the newlywed game? You guys need to start taking notes and getting to know each other for the interview! This will be good practice and fun."

Without hesitation David replies, "Yes, that sounds very fun. Let's do this?" Rona chimes in with a raised hand, "What if we make it interesting?"

An inquisitive Kathrina asks, "Interesting?"

Rona explains, "Yes, break out that tequila bottle I saw in the kitchen. With every wrong answer, someone has to take a shot!"

David is all game now. He says, "Bring it on!" Concerned about Rona driving under the influence, Kathrina urges Rona to spend the night. Rona agrees with Kathrina and attempts to call Shirley to inform her of their plans. Shirley, however, does not respond. After multiple attempts to contact her via phone, Rona leaves her a voicemail and then follows it up with a text message stating, "Hi babe, I am going to spend the night at David and Kathrina's house.

We will prepare for the DHS interview and take pictures at breakfast in the morning." Rona puts her phone on charge and is now primed for the challenge of newlywed trivia questions.

Rona and David sit directly across from each other with Kathrina sitting between them as the host of the game. To begin, Kathrina states that each participant should write their answer on the notepads in front of them and that for every wrong answer a shot must be consumed. She asks them both to write legibly and to include the questions asked so that they can reference these notes later when preparing for the DHS interview. Kathrina says we will start with a few easy questions, "What would be your spouse's ideal date?"

David and Rona write down their answers. Rona asks to answer first, confident she has the correct answer, "Go see the Lakers play!"

David lifts his notepad to display his answer, "I put go to a sports event."

Kathrina also plays the judge and agrees the answers are close enough to continue without Rona taking a shot. Now its David's turn; he guesses that Rona would respond, "Go hiking."

She raises her notepad and it reads, "Dinner and a movie."

Kathrina yells out, "Shots shots shots. GO David!"

While David is halfway through his shot, Kathrina asks Rona, "What kind of movie?"

Rona replies, "Romantic comedy. I think love has a unique sense of humor and that for two people to really enjoy each other they have to be able to laugh at each other and the challenges they face without judgment or fear."

David states, "That's too deep! Next question please?"

Question after question, Rona and David are becoming very acquainted with each other and the alcohol is removing all inhibition. Each answer is raw and unadulterated. Kathrina, the emcee of the show, digs deeper and deeper with each question into Rona's personality, likes, wants, and dreams. David is losing badly, and the shots are starting to have a pronounced impact on his consciousness. Mercilessly, Kathrina selects questions that favor female intuition. Rona is tipsy, but fully aware of Kathrina's intentions and a willing participant in sharing her deepest secrets to Kathrina know that David will likely not remember the night. David's inebriation leaves Rona and Kathrina with full control to guide the conversation where they see fit without scrutiny or suspicions about their intentions.

David's speech begins to slur, and he has obviously had enough. He can no longer coherently respond to Kathrina's inquiries and he concedes to Rona. Now a sloppy drunk, he exerts a full effort to communicate his desire to be a hospitable host and a gentleman, he stammers, "I'll…I'll just sleep here. Rona yoooooou are the champ. Take my bed!"

He grabs a pillow from the couch and before anyone can react to his actions, he's snoring like a hibernating bear."

Kathrina and Rona are utterly amused and giggle like hyenas; conscious, that together, their estrogen has trumped David's testosterone.

Rona is taller and too husky to fit into any of Kathrina's sweats or pjs. Kathrina jokes, "Here you can wear a pair of David's basketball shorts. He's always bragging about how comfortable they are for bed. Your ass is too big for my PJs."

Rona laughs and replies, "Basketball shorts have always been my favorite sleep wear. I like to go commando."

The two break out in an uncontrolled laughter that likely causes Mr. Bradshaw in the front house to roll over in bed.

In bed, Kathrina is accustomed to sleeping with the lamp on the bedside table illuminated.

Rona inquires, "Are you going to turn off the light?"

Kathrina replies, "Does it bother you?"

Rona being mischievous responds, "Yes, I can't sleep with lights on. Why do you need it? I'm right here! I will protect you."

Kathrina now blushing and grinning from ear to ear, reaches over to extinguish the light. Settling into her usual space in the bed, Kathrina now looking into the glimmer of light reflecting in Rona's eyes, Kathrina inquires, "Who is going to kiss me goodnight? I'm the opposite of Sleeping Beauty. I cannot sleep until someone kisses me."

Without hesitation Rona lunges forward and gently lands a kiss on Kathrina's lips. Kathrina responds with a slight nibble on Rona's upper lip and then just as quickly as the kiss began it ends in slight discomfort and embarrassment. Kathrina and Rona each wish each other a goodnight. Kathrina being accustomed to having some sort of physical contact with David in bed reaches out and caresses Rona's limp hand.

At the breakfast table, Rona is blown away by Kathrina efforts to prepare a traditional Filipino breakfast. David is spoiled and totally oblivious to the love that is infused in Kathrina's cooking. Katrina prepares a traditional dish called longsilog, fried rice with sweet sausage and eggs. With each bite into the longsilog, Rona has to hold back urges to comment on her appreciation for such a well-prepared meal. Holding back the words, doesn't stop her face from communicating to Kathrina that she has done a remarkable job. As everyone's tummy's fill, there is a shift in focus from physical sustenance to financial stability. The group decides that it will be important for Rona and David to have a joint bank account. David and Kathrina will deposit the funds for each progress payment and the final payment to this account. It will create the illusion that David and Rona are saving money together. They will close their current mobile phone accounts so that they can open a family plan. They will use Rona's address on the base as their home residence. Rona will enroll David on her medical, dental and vision insurance plan with the Department of Defense. They plan a date to file the adjustment of status paperwork with the Department of Homeland Security and a date to transfer the next progress payment. For David and Kathrina the road map to citizenship is set and for Rona the path to financial freedom is evident.

Rona returns home after a long day at work and finds a note from Shirley. The note reads, "Hey Melly Baby, the kids are visiting their father. I am going out with some old friends from high school. Please don't stay up for me. I'll join you in bed later tonight and talk to you in the morning. I ordered Chinese for you and left it in the fridge. Please enjoy."

Rona, not impressed at all and immediately suspicious, begins to search the house for potential clues of what could be going on. After eating her Chinese food and dressing for bed, her idle mind becomes the devil's workshop and she grabs Shirley's iPad. Shirley is not aware, but Rona has closely monitored Shirley using he iPad and knows the profile password. She logs into the account and goes directly to Shirley's Instagram account to check her DMs.

Among the DMs to her family, Rona finds messages to multiple men who appear to be serving on the same base. This discovery is no surprise to Rona. Though she feels a slight sting, she expected it. Looking through the messages she finds nude images exchanged between Shirley and the kid's soccer coach. It doesn't take much effort for her to ascertain that Shirley has met up with the soccer coach for a sexual escapade at a beachside motel. Instead of confronting Shirley, she sends a text to Kathrina subconsciously searching for sympathy and affection.

David and Kathrina are enjoying a long-awaited date at the movie theater. The latest marvel super hero movie has been released and David can't resist seeing them immediately. As the lights dim in the theater, Kathrina could care less about the excitement surrounding the move and is more concerned about the company in her presence and her need for affectionate care. She reaches to hold David's hand but its digging deep in the popcorn bucket, his other hand filled with red vines, she settles for a little space of real estate on his shoulder to rest her head. David is so entranced and pumped up about the super hero movie that he doesn't even feel Kathrina head resting on his shoulder. Not even remotely interested in following the plot, Kathrina checks her phone in her purse and sees that she has multiple missed calls from Rona and an unread text message. Curious to figure out what's going on she puts her phone in her purse to contain the bright light and reads the text from Rona.

It reads, "Hey buddy. Where are you? I need your company."

With the phone still in her purse Kathrina responds, "I'm here at the movies with David. He's being a dick. It's like he doesn't even realize I'm here. I could be making out with the person next to me and he wouldn't even know."

Rona replies, "Sorry Kathrina, I wish I were there. I'd appreciate your company. Please text or call me after your movie finishes."

David is still pumped up about the movie as they are walking to the car to go home. He is making forecasts about the next episode having watch the post credit teasers. Kathrina isn't at all amused. In fact, she changes the subject drastically, stating, "Babe, I came to watch this movie with you. My birthday is coming up. Can we please go to Disneyland!" Knowing that David detests almost every aspect of attending an amusement park, she's hopeful that by giving in to his desires to see the super hero movie that he will be accommodating of her request to attend Disneyland, the happiest place on earth. David is quick to express his distaste for lines, crowds and all the walking. Kathrina pleading, "But babe it's my birthday!"

David replies, I need to drive Uber this weekend to ensure that we have enough money for our next progress payment. How about I give you a little cash and you go shopping to get those shoes you wanted? Call Jennifer, I'm sure she would love to go with you. Friday nights yield the best fares of the week. I will take you to dinner Saturday night and we can celebrate your birthday."

Lying in bed staring at the ceiling trying to find a pattern in the popcorn texture, Kathrina decides to call Rona back while David showers. Rona answers the call on the first ring, "Hello friend, thanks for calling me."

Kathrina replies, "The pleasure is mine. I miss you. Are you ok?"

Rona answers, "Not really, but I'm happy to be talking to you. It helps me forget the pain and betrayal."

Kathrina inquires with a sympathetic tone, "What's wrong Rona?"

Rona goes into details about the nude pictures and flirtatious messages that she found in Shirley's Instagram account. She explains to Kathrina that this discovery verifies her suspicions. Trying her best to connect with Rona as a fellow victim of being taking for granted, Kathrina responds, "My birthday is Friday. I asked David for one simple gift. Take me to Disneyland. He would rather give me money to go shopping and drive Uber than spend time doing the one thing I want to do on my birthday."

Recognizing that she isn't alone in her suffering, Rona exclaims, "Fuck them both! Let's go Disneyland. Me and you!"

It's Friday and David has fulfilled two fares. He's confident the day is going to be very productive as he drives through Hollywood searching for his next fare. Driving past the Capitan Theater he is reminded of Kathrina's desire to go to Disneyland by the feature presentation, Sleeping Beauty. He is instantly overcome with a sense of guilt and disappointment in his lack of empathy for Kathrina's desires. He begins concocting a plan to treat Kathrina to a wonderful evening. He rushes to her favorite restaurant and picks out her favorite dishes, then he stops by the Redbox to rent the latest Disney release. To top things off he runs in to Costco just before closing time to pick up a cake that is Disney themed and purchases prepaid gift cards to attend the park.

Rushing home, he wants to prepare the surprise for Kathrina before she gets home from shopping. He decorates the living room with streamers from their closet and blows up festive colored balloons to adorn the living room. Party planning is not his specialty, but he is determined to please Kathrina. The final touch is the lighting of the candles and selection of background music. He is convinced that everything is perfect, but now he's wondering where's Kathrina. Knowing he only gave her $150.00 bucks he is surprised that she has not returned home from shopping. He sends her text after text, with growing anxiety that she is extremely angry with him for choosing to work on her birthday. Pacing the floor and peeking out of the window with an OCD fervor, he is finally relieved to see a car pulling up into the driveway. However, the car is not Jennifer's. He is surprised to see that Rona has brought his birthday girl home.

Sitting in the driveway and exhausted from the long day, Kathrina doesn't know how to express her gratitude to Rona for making her birthday one to remember. She looks to Rona and before she can say thank you a tear of joy runs down her cheek.

She states, "Rona, I had so much fun with you. More than I have had in so long. You don't have any idea what this means to me."

Rona replies, "I feel lucky to have had the opportunity to share this special day with you." Her emotions amplified by the moment, Kathrina can no longer resist the urge to express her romantic feelings for Rona. She caresses Rona's hand, their eyes lock, and their heads drift toward each other under extreme magnetic attraction as Kathrina initiates a soft kiss expressing her appreciation. The veil of inhibition drops suddenly and the two are locked in a passionate embrace filled with lovingly, lustful kisses.

David stands at the window in utter disbelief, rubbing his eyes to make sure he is truly seeing what he sees. As the reality sinks in, his heart sinks and grows cold while emotions of both betrayal and guilt tug at his being.

Chapter 10 The Break Up

David represses his emotions and though his heart is burdened with the revelation that he has lost Kathrina's affection he doesn't confront her. Thinking of and rationalizing all the possible outcomes of a confrontation doesn't resonate in his heart with any positive consequence. He instead pushes forward with the "original sin," pursuing his legal adjustment of status through the fictitious, unholy matrimony. His heart is frozen and retreats into a shell like a hermit crab. He's back to playing his video games, basketball with the boys and focuses on earning income driving Uber. Kathrina is so enraptured by the flame of passion burning between her and Rona that she is blind to any changes in David's dealings with her. To her, their household is status quo - her romantic needs now satisfied and her American Dream in process.

Driving Uber late on a Saturday evening, David is hoping to pick up some fares that might help bring some cheer into his life. Though he has been repressing his feelings, there are days that depression rises from his gut like indigestion after eating a spicy chili with extra onions. Saturday night fares usually expose him to the young fun seeking crowds that are excited and full of life. After dropping off a rambunctious group of drunk ladies, he heads back to the club scene in Hollywood. On his way back to score another fare, he gets a notification to accept a fare. He accepts the fare and is not impressed because it's for someone waiting at one of the local hospitals. He needs the fare and being new to Uber he is working on building his rating, so he doesn't want to cancel it. David tries to prepare himself mentally and emotionally for the prospects of picking up a sad or sickly guest. He places a fresh box of tissue papers in the backseat just in case.

As he approaches the hospital pick-up zone he notices that there are many people waiting and that there is no place to park because there are Uber, Lyft and cab drivers monopolizing the curbside area. The security guard responsible for directing traffic is visibly fatigued and yielding to the aggressive drivers. David drives by slowly trying to find a place to squeeze in, when suddenly his rear passenger door is opened, and he slams on his brakes. He looks back and there is a beautiful nurse peeking into his car greeting him by name, "Hello David?"

He stutters, "Uh…Uh yes, I'm David." She replies, "I'm Riza."

David is virtually frozen in the moment and Riza's smile is like an oasis adorning the sands of a cold lonely desert. David throws the car in park and jumps out of the car to run over and greet Riza. Like a vagabond who has been wandering in the desert, he is amazed to find that Riza is not a mirage. He is "thirsty," but careful not wanting to freak her out. He is smiling and especially hospitable, offering her water and closing her door as she sits in the backseat of his car. Riza smiles and is very thankful, but also fatigued and seemingly sad.

Now en route to Riza's destination, David is intrigued and very curious to know more about Riza. He inquires, "Is the music ok?"

Riza replies, "Could you please turn it down a little? I'm not really in the mood."

David quickly adjust the volume and digs deeper, "I'm sorry."

Looking in his rear-view mirror he notices that she has tears in her eyes and that she appears to be on her phone.

Still wanting to make a connection with her, he inquires, "Would you like to use my charger for your phone?"

Riza responds, "No thank you. I'd probably be happier if my phone just died."

David replies, "Oh, I'm sorry! Are you ok? Can I get anything for you or make any stops on our way to your destination?"

Riza, noticing that David is sincerely interested in her grief and knowing that she will not receive comfort from anyone in her cold, dark apartment, decides to open up about her problems, "No thank you. I just had a really rough day."

David responds, "I can only imagine the patience you need to help people experiencing pain and suffering on a daily basis. I have the highest respect for nurses."

Smiling, Riza blushes and states, "Thank you. It makes me happy to help people; that's not what has me down tonight."

David waits patiently, hoping Riza will volunteer the source of her grief. After a few moments of awkward silence, David inquires, "Do you want to talk about it?" Riza responds with the intensity of a dormant volcano that has been building pressure for eons: "Today I found out my boyfriend is gay! We had been dating for nearly 6 years and I thought I would marry him. Instead, I found out that he has been in the closet for years. He has been living a double life and has finally decided that he needs to be with a man to be happy. I feel so betrayed!"

David responds, "Oh my God, that's devastating. How could any guy choose another man over you? You are so beautiful." Riza replies, "Thank you David." David, feeling that this is his opportunity to connect, responds using his personal experience with Kathrina as leverage, "Betrayal seems to be in the air these days."

Pulling up to Riza's destination, she inquires before stepping out of the car, "What do you mean?"

David explains, "You boyfriend chose a man over you. My fiancé chose a woman over me. I caught them kissing a couple of weeks ago."

Riza's jaw drops and she says, "That's insane. I'm sorry. You seem like a really sweet guy. I guess we have something in common."

David quickly replies, "Yes we do. I'd love to see if we have more in common."

Without hesitation Riza offers David her phone number and tells him to call her anytime. Driving to his next fare, David is in disbelief about Riza. He pulls over for a moment to send a text to the number she gave him almost as a test of reality, challenging the cognition that her existence is nothing more than a figment of his imagination. He types in the number and send a simple text, "Good night Riza. This is David. It was a pleasure to meet you."

Riza replies instantly, "The pleasure was mine. Thanks for allowing me to unload my drama on you."

David replies, "Anytime you need someone to be your dump, please call me!"

Riza responds with a happy face emoji, the poo emoji and suggests, "You better get a big shovel! Text me whenever. I need to sleep now. Sooo tired."

Over the next several weeks, David and Riza exchange text messages and phone calls with increasing regularity. David's dependence on video games fades! His desire to play basketball with the boys has passed. Now he spends countless hours at night driving Uber as a cover for him to get to know Riza better. The two text each other constantly and eventually begin to meet for coffee on a nightly basis in the hospital coffee shop. Kathrina is in a fog with regard to her relationship with David. He comes home late almost every night and is up early sitting on the couch drinking coffee and ready to start his day with Mr. Bradshaw. She, however, is not bothered by the lack of attention and affection that she is getting from David. Instead her time and focus are squarely on Rona. Though connected through the arrangement of the holy matrimony, physically and emotionally, they both drift further and further apart from each other without effort or regret. They have grown romantically independent of each other and are essentially nothing more than roommates sharing expenses. Kathrina takes advantage of the time that David is out driving to connect with Rona. More often than not, Rona is at their place by the time David gets home. She is there under the guise of building their case for immigration. They snap pictures and review details for their upcoming interviews. Though obvious and clear that her true intentions are to be with Kathrina, the idea remains unspoken. David no longer cares, as he is happy to be out and available to his new crush, Riza.

Shirley waking up as Rona climbs into the bed, rolls over to hug Rona. As she is caressing Rona she notices that the embrace is not reciprocated with the same level of passion. Rona's arms are limp. Then she notices something extremely extraordinary and inquires, "Are you wearing perfume?"

Rona without hesitation replies, "Hell no. You know I don't wear that stuff."

Shirley doesn't bite her tongue, "You smell like Kathrina! Why?"

Rona doesn't respond; she rolls over to sleep as if the question was never asked. However, Shirley doesn't yield in her efforts to cross-examine Rona, her questioning persists, "After all the time you spend over there, where is our next payment? You promised that I would get my breast augmentation with the next payment! What is going on?"

Rona just lies there in silence. Shirley, becoming annoyed, nudges Rona stating, "Well? Where is my money?"

Jumping out of bed, Rona's face is red and she's fuming with anger. Like a levee giving way to flash flood, Rona erupts, "Fuck you Shirley! I'm not giving you shit. Let one of your boyfriends buy them for you! Yes, I smell like perfume because I've been sleeping with Kathrina! I am done with your shit. I deserve better!" Shirley lies in bed speechless as Rona storms out of the room to sleep on the couch.

In the morning, Rona and Shirley agree to separate. Rona gives Shirley a couple hundred dollars and wishes her luck. While Rona is out to work, Shirley calls her latest sugar daddy over to help her pack up so that she and the kids can move in with her mother. Rona, receiving a text from Shirley stating that she left the spare key under the front door mat, feels the weight of an elephant being lifted from her chest. Despite still having to face her financial obstacles, she has not had a feeling of freedom and happiness this grand since she left home to join the Airforce.

Growing tired of sneaking around to meet with David late at night, Riza inquires over coffee with David, "How long do we have to sneak around? Why are you even with her? Aren't we happy together?"

David replies, "What about my citizenship?"

Riza laughs, "Don't be a dummy. I'm a citizen and I am single! Let's be together for real!"

David in disbelief asks, "Are you proposing to me?"

Finally, in an imperative tone, Riza exclaims "Marry me you fool!"

Like a contestant from the game show "Let's Make a Deal" that has been called down to play, David cannot contain his emotions. He springs to his feet practically spilling his coffee and gives Riza a hug that nearly breaks her back. He gives her a multitude of cheesy kisses while she is still calmly and calculatingly detailing the rules for the next round of play.

She states, "You will go home to your lesbian fiancé and tell her you will not continue to live like this. You will tell her that you will not continue to pay for this bogus marriage and that you will proceed to file a divorce immediately. Tell them that they can have the down payment! You will gather all your belongings and move in with me."

David without hesitation agrees with the deal. He could care less to find out what options are behind door numbers two and three. That night David sleeps peacefully, dreaming of his future with Riza.

In the morning he is anxious to reveal the deal to Kathrina, but it is Thanksgiving day and both of them have made plans for dinner – just not with each other. Kathrina tells David that she is going to have dinner with Carl and Jennifer, where she will secretly plan to meet Rona. David tells Kathrina that he is going to have dinner with Ranjith and Arlene; where he will secretly plan to meet Riza. The two are very nonchalant in the delivery of their plans and there are no hard feelings or emotions attached to the idea of spending the holiday in separate places.

David and Riza have a blast watching football and eating thanksgiving dinner. Arlene and Ranjith, who are now engaged, quickly form a bond with the new couple. They sense a relationship of transparently innocent love and affection. Watching David and Riza together reminds them of their first moments together. Arlene is concerned about her friend Kathrina but believes that David deserves to be happy too. She gives the relationship her stamp of approval and wishes David and Riza the best in their pursuit of happiness together. That night following dinner, David does not return home. Instead he "consummates" a relationship and future with Riza. The two make passionate love all night long as if it were their honeymoon. Together, they are transported to David's imaginative oasis. They are in paradise and there is nothing that exists outside of their realm of imagination and pleasure.

The sun rises on "Black Friday" and Kathrina realizes that David didn't come home. There are no sounds of video games coming from his man cave. No loud singing coming from the shower in their bathroom. The silence is virtually deafening as she panics thinking that something must have happened to him driving back from Arlene's. She grabs his phone to ring him, but just as it starts to ring she can hear someone coming through the front door. She runs down the hall afraid of what discovery awaits. She exclaims, "David where are you been? I was worried sick. I didn't realize that you didn't come home!" Calmly, David replies, "I'm fine everything is ok, but we need to talk."

Sitting at the kitchen counter, David explains, "Kathrina, I know there is something between you and Rona. We have drifted apart and I have found someone who makes me happy."

Ironically, the one aspiration that they thought would bring them closer together has driven them further apart. Kathrina responds, "You are right, we will never fulfill our dreams if we continue along this path."

David continues, "We can fulfill our dreams, just not with each other. You have Rona. I will divorce her so that you can continue your pursuit for citizenship with her. My new friend will help me."

In that immediate moment, Kathrina feels defeated. David embraces her and gently kisses her forehead stating, "Don't be sad. In the end, we will be happy."

Book 2 coming soon…

www.ingramcontent.com/pod-product-compliance
Lightning Source LLC
Chambersburg PA
CBHW071455030726
47593CB00003B/1017